The Winds of Darkover

He was standing on a stretch of soft grass; it was night, but it was not dark. All around him the night flamed and roared with a great fire, reaching in tendrils of ravening flame far above his head. And in the midst of the flame there was a woman.

Woman?

She was almost inhumanly tall and slender, but girlish; she stood bathed in the flame as if standing carelessly under a waterfall. The flames were licking around her face and her flame–colored hair. And then the girlish, merry face wavered and became supernally beautiful with the beauty of a great goddess burning endlessly in the fire, a kneeling woman bound in golden chains . . .

Also in Arrow by Marion Zimmer Bradley

THE DARKOVER NOVELS:

The Winds of Darkover

Marion Zimmer Bradley

A Darkover novel

ARROW BOOKS

Arrow Books Limited
62–65 Chandos Place, London WC2N 4NW

An imprint of Century Hutchinson Limited

London Melbourne Sydney Auckland
Johannesburg and agencies throughout
the world

First published in Great Britain 1978
Reprinted 1987

Printed and bound in Great Britain by
Anchor Brendon Limited, Tiptree, Essex

ISBN 0 09 917810 9

1

Barron dumped the last of his gear into a duffel bag, pulled the straps tight, and said to nobody in particular, 'Well, that's that and the hell with all of them.'

He straightened, taking a last look around the neat, tight little world of spaceport living-quarters. Built to conserve materials (it had been the first Terran building on Dark-over, in the zone later to become Trade City), it had something in common with a spaceship's cabin; it was narrow, bright, clean and cramped, the furniture functional and almost built-in. It would have suited a professional spaceman perfectly. Ground crews were another matter; they tended to get claustrophobia.

Barron had complained as much as anyone else, saying the place might be a decent fit for two mice, if one of them were on a stiff diet. But now that he was leaving it, he felt a curious pang, almost homesickness. He had lived here five years.

Five years! I never meant to stick to one planet that long!

He hoisted the duffel bag to his shoulder and closed the door of his quarters for the last time.

The corridor was as functional as the living quarters; reference charts and maps papered the walls up to the height of a tall man's eye level. Barron strode along, not seeing the familiar charts, but he did cast a brief bitter glance at the dispatch board, seeing his name there in red on the dreaded rep-sheet. He had five reps – official reprimands – when seven would put one out of the Space Service for good.

And no wonder, he thought. *I didn't get any dirty deal; in fact, they went easy on me. Pure luck, and no credit to me, that cruiser and the mapping ship didn't crash and blow the damned spaceport right off Darkover, and half Trade City with them!*

He set his mouth tight. Here he was, worrying about demerits like a kid in school – and yet it wasn't merely that. Many people in Terran Space Service went through their whole twenty years without a single rep – and he'd piled up five in one disastrous night.

Even though it wasn't his fault.

Yes it was, damn it. Who else could I blame it on? I should have reported sick.

But I wasn't sick!

The rep–sheet read: gross neglect of duty, grave danger of causing accident to a landing spacecraft. They had found him literally napping on duty. *But damn it, I wasn't asleep either!*

Daydreaming?

Try telling them that. Try telling them that when your every nerve and muscle should have been alert over the all-important dispatch board, you were – somewhere else. You were caught up in a deep dream, bewildered with colors, sights, sounds, smells, blazes of brilliance. You were leaning into an icy wind, under a deep purple sky, a blaze of red sunlight overhead – the Darkovan sun – the sun that the Terrans called The Bloody Sun. But you'd never seen it like that, reflected in rainbow prisms through a great wall of crystalline glass. You heard your own boots ringing on ice-hard stone – and your pulse was pounding with hate, and you felt the surge of adrenalin in your blood. You broke into a run, feeling the hatred and blood-lust rise to a crest inside you; before you something reared up – man, woman, beast – you hardly knew or cared – and you heard your own snarl as a whip came crashing down and something screamed –

The dream had dissolved in the thundering nightmare noise of klaxons, the all-quarters alarm of sirens and whoopers and bells, the WRECK lights blazing everywhere, and your reflexes took over. You'd never moved so fast. But it was too late. You had slammed the wrong button and the dispatch tower was fouled up by that all-important eight-second margin, and only a minor miracle of seat-of-the-pants navigation by the young captain of the mapping ship – he was getting three medals for it – had saved *the spaceport authority from the kind of disaster that waked people up – what people were left – in screeching nightmares for twenty years afterward.*

Nobody had wasted words on Barron since. His name on the rep-sheet had made him a pariah. He had been told to vacate his quarters by 2700 that night and report for a new assignment, but nobody bothered telling him where. It was as simple as that – five years in Darkover Spaceport and seventeen in the service had been wiped out. He didn't feel especially mistreated. There wasn't room in the Terran Spaceforce for that kind of mistake.

The corridor ended in an archway; a plaque, which Barron ignored after seeing it every day for years, told him he was now in Central Coordinating. Unlike the building where quarters were located, this one was constructed of native Darkovan stone, translucent and white as alabaster, with enormous glass windows. Through them he could see flaring, blue spaceport lights, the shapes of groundcraft and resting ships, and, far beyond the lights, pale greenish moonlight. It was half an hour before dawn. He wished he'd stopped for some breakfast; then he was glad he hadn't. Barron wasn't thin-skinned, but the way the men ignored him in the cafeteria would put anyone off his food. He hadn't bothered eating much in the last couple of days.

There was always the Old Town, the Darkovan part of Trade City where he sometimes slipped away for exotic food when he was tired of the standard fare of the quarters; there were not a few restaurants which catered to spacemen and tourists who came for 'exotic delicacies'. But he hadn't felt like trying to pass the guards; he might have been stopped. They might have thought he was trying to escape an offical process. He wasn't officially under arrest, but his name was mud.

He left the duffel bag outside the narrow bank of elevators, stepped in and pressed the topmost button. The elevator soared up, depositing him outside the dispatch room. He lowered his head, passing it without a glance inside and headed for the coordinator's office in the pent-house.

And then, without warning – he was standing on a high parapet, winds flowing icily around his body, ripping at him with enough force to tear his clothes off, ridging his skin with gooseflesh and pain. Below him, men screamed and moaned and died over the sounds of clashing steel; and somewhere he heard stone falling with a great crunching rumble like the end of the world. He could not see. He clung hard to the stone, feeling frost bite with fiery teeth at his stiff fingers, and fought the sickness rising in his throat. *So many men. So many dead, all of them my people and my friends* . . .

He let go of the stone. His fingers were so cramped that he had to pry them off with his other hand. He caught his blowing garments around him, feeling an instant of incongruous physical comfort in the thick fur against his cold hands, and went swiftly, on groping feet, through the blind dark. He moved as in a dream, knowing where he was going without knowing why; his feet knew the familiar path. He felt them move from flagstone to wood parquet to thick carpeting, then down a long flight of stairs and up another flight – farther and farther, until the distant sounds of battle and falling walls were muffled and finally silenced. His throat was thick and he sobbed as he went. He passed through a low archway, automatically ducking his head against the stone arch he had never seen and would never see. A current of chill air blew on him. He fumbled in the darkness for something like a loose hood of feathery textures; he drew it downward swiftly and he thrust his head through the feathers, pulling it down.

He felt himself falling back and in the same instant he seemed to rise, to soar upward and swoop outward on the wings of the feathery substance. The darkness suddenly thinned and was gone, and light broke around him – not through his darkened eyes, but through the very skin of his body – and he felt cold reddish light and frosty clouds. Weightless, borne on the feather dress, he soared outward, guiding himself through the sudden brilliance of dawn.

Quickly he grew accustomed to the bird dress, and balancing on one wing (*It's a long time since I dared to do this.*)

he turned to look below.

The colors were strange, flat, shapes distorted and concave; he was not seeing them with ordinary mortal eyes. Far below a swarm of men in rough, dark clothing clustered around a rude tower covered in skins, next to an outwork. Arrows flew, men screamed; on the wall a man toppled with a long despairing shriek, and fell out of his sight. He beat harsh pinions, trying to swoop down, and . . .

He was standing on firm flooring, wiping the sweat of terror from his face.

He was here. He was Dan Barron. He was not flying bodiless except for a few feathers over a weird tipping landscape, fighting a biting current of wind. He stared at his fingers and put one into his mouth. It felt numb, frostbitten. *The stone was cold.*

It had happened again.

It was so real, *so damnably real*. His skin was still gooseflesh and he mopped eyes still streaming from the bitter wind. *Good God*, he thought, and shuddered. Had someone been slipping him hallucinogenic drugs? Why would anyone do that? He had no enemies, as far as he knew. He had no real friends – he wasn't the type to make them at a strange outpost – but no enemies either. He did his work and minded his own business, and he knew no one who envied him either his few possessions or the tough and somewhat underpaid job he had been doing. The only explanation was that he was mad, psychotic, freaked-out, off his landing base. He realized that in that weird dream, obsession or hallucination, he had been speaking and thinking in Darkovan – the strong accented mountain Darkovan which he understood, but could not speak except for the few words necessary to order a meal or buy some knickknack in Trade City. He shivered again and mopped his face. His feet had carried him within a few feet of the coordinator's office, but he stopped, trying to get his breath and his bearings.

This made five times.

The first three times had struck him as abnormally vivid

daydreams, born of boredom and hangover and based on his infrequent but colorful excursions into the Old Town. He had dismissed them without much thought, even though he woke shuddering with the reality of the surges of fear or hatred which possessed him in these dreams. The fourth – the fourth had been the near-catastrophe of the spaceport. Barron wasn't an imaginative man. His possible explanations went as far as a nervous breakdown, or someone with a grudge slipping him a hallucinatory drug as a grim joke, and not a step further. He wasn't paranoid enough to think that someone had done it for the purpose it achieved, his disgrace and a spaceport catastrophe. He was confused, a little scared and a little angry, but not sure if the anger was his own or part of the strange dream.

He couldn't continue to delay. He waited a minute more, then straightened his shoulders and knocked at the coordinator's door. A light flashed a green COME IN, and he stepped in.

Mallinson, Coordinator of Spaceport Activities for the Terran zone of Darkover, was a hefty man who looked, at any hour of day or night, as if he'd slept in his uniform. He appeared unimaginative and serious. Any notion Barron might have had about revealing his experiences to his superior died unspoken. Nevertheless, Mallinson looked straight at Barron, and he was the first person who'd done so for five days.

Without preamble he said, 'All right, what the hell happened? I pulled your file; you're listed as a damned good man. In my experience, men don't pile up a perfect record and then rack it up like *that*; the man who's heading for a big mistake starts out by making dozens of little mistakes first, and we have time to pull him off the spot before he really piles something up. Were you sick? Not that it's an excuse – if you were you should have reported and requested a relief man. We expected to find you dead of a heart attack – we didn't think anything else would slow you down like that.'

Barron thought about the dispatcher's room and its enormous board which patterned all traffic in and out of this spaceport. Mallinson said, not giving him time to answer, 'You don't drink or drug. You know, most men last about eight months on the dispatch board; then the responsibility starts giving them nightmares, they start making little fumbles, and we pull them off and transfer them. When you never made even a little fumble, we should have realized that you just didn't have sense enough – the little fumbles are the mind's way of yelling for help, yelling "This is too much for me, get me out of here." When you didn't, we should have pulled you off anyway. That's why you weren't cashiered, kicked out with seven reps, and slapped with a millicred fine. We left you on the board five years, and we should have known we were asking for trouble.'

Barron realized that Mallinson hadn't expected any answer. People who made mistakes of that caliber never could explain why. If they'd known why they would have guarded against it.

'With your record, Barron, we could transfer you out to the Rim, but we have an opening here; I understand you speak Darkovan?'

'Trade City language. I understand the other, but I fumble in it.'

'Even so. Know anything about mapping and exploring?' Barron jumped. It had been a ship from M & E which had nearly crashed five days ago, and that sector was in his mind, but a second glance at Mallinson convinced him that the man was simply asking for information, not needling. He said, 'I've read a book or two on xenocartography – no more.'

'Lens grinding?'

'The principles. Most kids make a small telescope some time or other; I did.'

'That's plenty. I didn't want an expert,' Mallinson said with a grim smile. 'We've got plenty of them, but it would put Darkovan backs up. Now, how much do you know about general Darkovan culture?'

Wondering where all this was leading, Barron said, 'Orientation Lectures Two, Three and Four, five years ago. Not that I've needed it much, working in the port.'

'Well then, you know the Darkovans never bothered a great deal with small technology – telescopes, microscopes and the like? Their supposed sciences go in other directions, and I don't know much about them either; nobody does except a few anthropologists and sociological experts. The facts remain; we, meaning the Board of Terran Affairs, sometimes get requests for minor technological help from individuals. Not from the government – if there is any government on Darkover, which I personally am inclined to doubt – but that's beside the point. Somebody or other out there, I'm not sure about the details, decided that for forest-fire control and fire watching, telescopes would be handy little gadgets to have around. Somehow the idea crawled up whatever channels it had to come through, and came to the Council of Elders in Trade City. We offered to sell them telescopes. Oh, no, they said politely, they'd rather have someone teach their men how to grind them, and to supervise their construction, installation and use. It's not the sort of thing we can send up a slip to Personnel for and find, just like that. But here you are, out of a job, and lens grinding listed in your comprehensive file as a hobby. Start today.'

Barron scowled. This was a job for an anthropologist, a liaison officer, a specialist in Darkovan language, or – *fire watching! Hell, that's a kid's job!* He said stiffly, 'Sir, let me remind you that this is out of my sector and out of my specialty. I have no experience in it. I'm a scheduling expert and dispatch man – '

'Not as of five days ago, you aren't,' Mallinson said brutally. 'Look, Barron, you're through in your own line; you know that. We don't want to ship you out in disgrace – not without some idea of what happened to you. And your contract isn't up for two years. We want to fit you in somewhere.'

There was nothing Barron could say to that. Resigning before a contract was up meant losing your holdback pay and your fee passage back to your home planet – which could strand you on a strange world and wipe out a year's pay. Technically he had a right to complain about being assigned outside his specialty field. But technically they had a right to fire him with seven reps, blacklist him, fine him, and press charges for gross negligence. He was getting a chance to come out of this – not clean, but not wrecked for good in the service.

'When do I start?' he asked. It was the only question he had left.

But he did not hear the answer. As he scanned Mallinson's face, suddenly it blurred.

He was standing on a stretch of soft grass; it was night, but it was not dark. All around him the night flamed and roared with a great fire, reaching in tendrils of ravening flame far above his head. And in the midst of the flame there was a woman.

Woman?

She was almost inhumanly tall and slender, but girlish; she stood bathed in the flame as if standing carelessly under a waterfall. She was not burning, not agonized. She looked merry and smiling. Her hands were clasped on her naked breasts, the flames licking around her face and her flame-colored hair. And then the girlish, merry face wavered and became supernally beautiful with the beauty of a great goddess burning endlessly in the fire, a kneeling woman bound in golden chains . . .

. . . 'and you can arrange all that downstairs in Personnel and Transportation,' Mallinson finished firmly, shoving back his chair. 'Are you all right, Barron? You look a bit fagged. I'll bet you haven't been eating or sleeping. Shouldn't you see a medic before you go? Your card is still good in Section 7. It's going to be all right, but the sooner you leave, the better. Good luck.' But he didn't offer to shake hands, and Barron knew it wasn't all right at all.

He stumbled over his own feet leaving the office, and the face of the burning woman, in its inhuman ecstasy, went with him in terror and amazement.

13

He thought, *what in the world – any world – has happened to me?*

And, in the name of all the gods of Earth, space and Darkover – why?

—— 2 ——

The breach in the outwork was being repaired.

Brynat Scarface had gone out to watch, and was standing on the inner parapet supervising the work. It was a cold morning and mists flowed up the mountainside; in the chill the men moved sluggishly. Little dark men from the mountains, most of them ragged and still battle-stained, fought the rough ground and the cold stone; they were moved by shouts and the occasional flick of a whip in the hands of one of Brynat's men.

Brynat was a tall man, dressed in ragged and slashed finery, over which he had drawn a fur cloak from the spoils of the castle. A great seamed scar ridged his face from eye to chin, giving to a face which had never been handsome the wolfish look of some feral beast which had somehow put on the dress of a man. At his heels his sword bearer, a little bat-eared man, scurried, bowing under the weight of the outlaw's sword. He cringed when Brynat turned to him, expecting a blow or a curse, but Brynat was in high good humor this morning.

'Fools we are, man – we spend days tearing down this wall,' he complained, 'and what is the first thing we do? We build it up again!'

The bat-eared man gave a nervous sycophant's laugh, but Brynat had forgotten his existence again. Drawing the fur around himself, he walked to the edge of the parapet and looked down at the ruined wall and the castle.

Storn Castle stood on a height defended by chasms and crags. Brynat knew he could congratulate himself for the feats of tactics and engineering which had broken the walls and poured men through them to storm the inner fortress.

Storn had been built in the old days to be impregnable, and impregnable it was and had remained through seven generations of Aldarans, Aillards, Darriels and Storns.

When it had housed proud lords of the Comyn – the old, powerful, psi–gifted lords of the Seven Domains of Darkover – it had been known to the world's end. Then the line had dwindled, outsiders had married into the remains of the families, and finally the Storns of Storn had come there. They had been peaceful lords without any pretense to be more than they were – wilderness nobility, gentle and honorable, living in peace with their tenants and neighbors, content to trade in the fine hunting hawks of the mountains and sell fine wrought metals from the forges of their mountain tribe, which dug ore from the dark cliffs and worked it at their fires. They had been rich and also powerful in their own way, if by power one meant that when word went forth from the Storn of Storn, men obeyed; but they smiled instead of trembling when they obeyed. They had little contact with the other mountain peoples and less with the lords of the farther mountains; they lived at peace and were content.

And now they had fallen.

Brynat laughed smugly. In their prideful isolation, the Storns could no longer even send for help to their distant lordly neighbors. With care, Brynat would be established here as lord of Storn Castle long before the word went out through the Hellers and the Hyades that Storn Castle had a new lord. And would they care that it was ruled no longer by Storn of Storn, but by Brynat of the Heights? He thought not.

A cold wind had come up, and the red sun was covered in scudding clouds. The men toiling at the lugged stones were moving faster now to keep warm in the biting wind, and a few flakes of snow were beginning to fall. Brynat jerked a careless shoulder at Bat–ears, and without looking to see if the little man followed – but woe to him if he hadn't – strode inside the castle.

Inside, far from watchers, he let his proud grin of triumph slide off. It had not been all victory, though his followers revelling in the rich spoil of the castle thought it had been. He sat in Storn's high seat, but victory eluded him.

He walked swiftly downward, until he came to a door padded with velvet and hung with curtains. Two of his mercenaries lolled here, drowsing on the comfort of cushions; an empty wineskin showed how they whiled away their guard. But they sprang up at the sound of his heavy tread, and one sniggered with the freedom of an old servitor.

'Ha, ha! Two wenches are better than one – hey, Lord?'

Seeing Brynat scowl the other said swiftly, 'No more weeping and wailing from the maid this morning, Lord. She is still, and we have not entered.'

Brynat scorned answer. He moved his hand imperiously and they flung open the door.

As the door hasp creaked, a small blue-clad form sprang up and whirled, long red braided hair flying about her shoulders. The face had once been piquantly lovely; now it was swollen and dark with bruises; one eye was half shut with a blow, but the other blazed in quenchless fury.

'You whelp of a bitch-wolf,' she said low, 'take one step further – I dare you!'

Brynat rocked back loosely on his heels, his mouth drawn to a wolfish smile. He set hands on hips and didn't speak, surveying the girl in blue. He saw the white, shaking hands, but noted that the swollen mouth did not tremble nor the eyes drop. He approved with inward laughter. Here he could feel genuine triumph.

'What, still unreconciled to my hospitality, Lady? Have I offered you word or deed of insult, or do you blame me for the roughness of my men in offering it?'

Her mouth was firm. 'Where is my brother? My sister?'

'Why,' he drawled, 'your sister attends my feasts nightly; I came to invite you to attend upon my lady wife this morning; I believe she pines for a familiar face. But, my Lady Melitta, you are pale; you have not touched the fine food I sent to you!' He made a low, burlesque bow and turned to pick up a tray laden with wine and rich food. He proffered it to her, smiling. 'See, I come in person, at your service –'

She took one step, snatched the tray, picked up a roast bird by one leg, and hurled it into his face.

Brynat swore, stepping backward and wiping the grease from his chin – with a great burst of laughter. 'Zandru's hells! *Damisela*, I should have taken you, not the whimpering, whining creature I chose!'

Breathing hard she surveyed him defiantly. 'I'd have killed you first.'

'I make no doubt you'd have tried! Had you been a man, the castle might never have fallen – but you wear skirts in place of hose and the castle lies in ruins and my men and I are here and all the smiths in Zandru's forges can't mend a broken egg. So I advise you in good sadness, little mistress: wash your face, and put on your fine robes, and attend on your sister, who is still Lady of Storn. If you have good sense, you'll advise her to have patience with her lot, and you shall both have robes and jewels and all things that women prize.'

'From you?'

'Who else?' he said with a laughing shrug, and flung the door open to the guards.

'The Lady Melitta is to come and go as she wills within the castle. But attend me, Mistress – the outworks, the parapets and the dungeons are forbidden, and I give my men leave – hear me well – to stop you by force if you attempt to go near them.'

She started to hurl a curse at him and then stopped herself, visibly toying with the thought of what even limited freedom could mean. At last she turned away without a word, and he shut the door and moved away.

Perhaps this would be the first step in his second victory. He knew, though his men did not, that Storn Castle conquered was only the first victory – and hollow without the second conquest. He bit off another curse, turned his back on the room prisoning the girl and strode on. Upward and upward he went, high into the old tower. Here there were no windows. There were only narrow slits which admitted, not the red daylight but a strange, eerie, flickering blue light like chained lightning. Brynat felt a strange, cold shiver pass over him.

Of ordinary dangers he was fearless. But this was the ancient Darkovan sorcery, the bare legends of which protected such places as Storn Castle long after their other defenses had fallen. Brynat clutched the amulet round his neck with suddenly nerveless fingers. He had guessed that the old magic was merely a show, had hardened his mercenaries to storm the castle and had won. He had caroused in Storn Castle and had laughed at the old tales. Their magic hadn't saved the castle, had it? He had thought it a show to frighten children, no more harmful than the northern lights.

He strode through the ghostly flickers, through a pale arch of translucent stone. Two of his hardened and brutal men, the most nerveless he could bribe to the task, lounged there on an old carven settee. He noted that they were neither gaming nor drinking, and that their eyes were averted from the arch beyond, where a flickering curtain of blue light played like a fountain between the stones. There was naked relief in their faces at sight of their chieftain.

'Any change?'

'None, Lord. The man's dead – dead as Durraman's donkey.'

'If I could believe that,' Brynat said between his teeth and strode boldly through the curtain of blue flame.

He had been through it before and it had been his bravest act – bold enough to dwarf the single-handed taking of the last barbican. He knew his men held him in awe for it, but this alone he did not fear. He had seen such things beyond the mountains; they were fearsome, indeed, but harmless. He felt and endured with distaste the electric tingle, the hairs bristling on head and forearms. He stiffened his backbone against the surge of animal fear and strode through.

The blue light died. He stood in a dark chamber, lit with a few pale tapers in fixed cressets; soft hangings of woven fur circled a single low couch, on which a man lay motionless.

The still form seemed to glow softly in the darkness; he was a slender, frail man, with pale hair streaming from a high forehead and deep-sunken eyes. Though he was still young, the face was drawn and stern. He wore a tunic and plain hose of woven silk, no furs and no jewels but a single star-shaped stone like an amulet around his neck. His hands looked white, soft, and useless – the hands of scribe or priest, hands which had never held a sword. The feet were bare and soft; the chest did not stir with breathing. Brynat felt the old frustrated fury as he looked down on the pale, soft-looking man. Storn of Storn lay there, helpless – yet beyond Brynat's reach.

His mind whirled him back to the hour of the castle's fall. The servants and soldiers had been seized and subdued; trusted men had been sent to bind, but not to harm, the ladies. The younger Storn, no more than a boy and bleeding from many wounds, Brynat had spared with grudging admiration – a boy to defend this castle alone? The lad was dungeoned, but Brynat's own surgeon had dressed his wounds. Storn of Storn was Brynat's real prey.

His men did not know; they had seen only the spoil of a rich house, the power of holding an ancient fortress where they could be secure. But Brynat sought choicer game: the talismans and powers of the old Storns. With Storn of Storn in his hands, a Storn of the true blood, he could wield them – and Storn, he had heard, was a fragile, sickly, unwarlike man – born blind. Hence had he lived in retirement, leaving the management of his castle to his young sisters and his brother. Brynat had maidens and boy; *now for the feeble Lord!*

He had found his way through weird lights and magical fire curtains to the private apartments of the Lord of Storn – and found him escaped; lying unrousable in trance.

And so he had lain for days. Now Brynat, sick with rage, bent over his couch, but no stir of muscle or breath revealed that the man lived.

'Storn!' he bellowed. It was a shout that he felt must

rouse even the dead.

No hair stirred. He might as well have howled into the winds around the parapet. Brynat, gritting his teeth, drew the skean from his belt. If he could not use the man, he held one power, at least: to send him from enchanted sleep to death. He raised the knife and brought it slashing down.

The knife turned in mid-air; it writhed, glowed blue, and exploded into white-hot flame from hilt to tip. Brynat howled in anguish, dancing about and shaking his burnt hand, to which the flowing skean clung with devilish force. The two mercenaries, trembling and bristling in the blue lights, faltered through the electrical curtain.

'You – you called us, *vai dom?*'

Savagely Brynat hurled the knife at them; it came unstuck and flew; one of them fumbled to catch it, yelled and shook it off to the floor, where it lay still hissing and sizzling. Brynat, with a low, savage stream of curses, strode from the chamber. The mercenaries followed, their eyes wide with terror and their faces like animal masks.

In marmoreal peace, far beyond their reach in unknowable realms, Storn slept on.

Far below, Melitta Storn finished bathing her bruised face. Seated before her toilet table, she concealed the worst of the marks with cosmetics, combed and braided her hair, and brought a clean gown from the press and donned it. Then, conquering a sudden spasm of sickness, she drank deeply of the wine on the tray. She hesitated a moment, then retrieved the roast bird from the floor, wiped it, and, deftly tearing it with her fingers, ate most of it. She did not wish Brynat's hospitality, but sick and faint with hunger she was useless to herself or her people. Now, with wine and food, she felt a measure of physical strength, at least, returning. Her mirror told her that except for swollen lip and darkened eye, she looked much as before.

And yet – nothing could ever be the same.

She remembered, shuddering, the walls crashing with a sound like the world's end; men surging from the gap; her youngest brother, Edric, bleeding from face and leg and white as a ghost after they tore him away from the last defenses; her sister Allira, screaming insanely as she fled from Brynat; the mad screams suddenly silenced in a cry of pain – then nothing. Melitta had run after them, fighting with bare hands and screaming, screaming until three men had seized and borne her, struggling like a trussed hen, to her own chamber. They had thrust her roughly within and barred the door.

She forced away the crowding memories. She had some freedom, now she must make use of it. She found a warm cape and went out of the room. The mercenaries at the door rose and followed her at a respectful, careful ten paces.

Apprehension throbbed in her, she walked through the deserted halls like a ghost through a haunted house, dogged by the steps of the strange brutes. Everywhere were the marks of siege, sack and ruin. Hangings were torn away, furniture hacked and stained. There were marks of fire and smoke in the great hall, and, hearing voices, she tiptoed past; Brynat's men caroused there and even if he had given orders to leave her alone, would drunken men heed?

Now, where is Allira?

Brynat, in hateful jesting – had he been jesting? – had referred to Allira as his lady wife. Melitta has been brought up in the mountains; even in these peaceful days she knew stories of such bandit invasions: castle sacked, men killed, lady forcibly married – if rape could be called marriage because some priest presided – announcement made that the bandit had married into the family and all was peaceful – on the surface. It was a fine subject for sagas and tales, but Melitta's blood ran cold at the thought of her delicate sister in that man's hands.

Where had Brynat taken her? Doubtless, to the old royal suite, furnished by her forefathers for entertaining the Hastur-Lords should they ever honor Storn Castle with their presence. That would be the sort of mixed blasphemy and conquest that would appeal to Brynat. Her heart racing, Melitta ran up the stairs, knowing suddenly what she would find there.

The royal suite was a scant four hundred years old; the carpeting felt new underfoot. The insignia of the Hasturs had been inlaid in sapphires and emeralds over the door, but hammer and pick had ripped the jewels from the wall and only broken stone remained.

Melitta burst into the room like a whirlwind, inner conviction – the old, seldom-used, half-remembered *knowing* inside her mind, the scrap of telepathic power from some almost-forgotten forefather – forcing her to look here for her sister. She sped through the rooms, hardly seeing the ravages of conquest there.

She found Allira in the farthest room. The girl was huddled in a window seat with her head in her arms, so quenched and trembling that she did not lift her head as Melitta ran into the room, but only cowered into a smaller and smaller bundle of torn silks. She started with a scream of weak terror as Melitta put a hand on her arm.

'Stop that, Allira. It's only me.'

Allira Storn's face was so bleared with crying that it was almost unrecognizable. She flung herself on the other girl, wrapped her arms round her, and burst into a hurricane of sobs and cries.

Melitta's heart quailed with sickening pity, but she grasped Allira firmly in both hands, held her off and shook her hard, until her head flapped loosely up and down. 'Lira, in Aldones' name, stop that squalling! That won't help you – or me, or Edric, or Storn, or our people! While I'm here, let's think. Use what brains you have left!'

But Allira could only gasp, 'He – he – huh – Buh – Brynat – ' She stared at her sister with such dazed, glassy eyes that Melitta wondered in a spasm of terror if harsh usage had left Allira witless or worse. If so, she was frighteningly alone, and might as well give up at once.

She freed herself, searched, and found on a sideboard a half-empty bottle of *firi*. She would rather have had water, or even wine, but in these straits anything would do. She dashed half the contents full into Allira's face. Eyes stung by the fiery spirits, Allira gasped and looked up; but now she saw her sister with eyes at least briefly sane. Melitta grasped her chin, tilted the bottle and forced a half-cup of the raw liquor down her sister's throat. Allira gulped, swallowed, coughed, choked, dribbled, then, anger replacing hysteria, struck down Melitta's arm and the cup.

'Have you lost your wits, Meli?'

'I was going to ask you that, but I didn't think you were in any shape to answer,' Melitta said vigorously. Then her voice became more tender. 'I didn't mean to frighten or hurt you, love; you've had more than enough of that, I know. But I had to make you listen to me.'

'I'm all right now – as much as I can ever be,' she amended, bitterly.

'You don't have to tell me,' Melitta said quickly, flinching from what she could read in her sister's mind; they were both wide open to each other. 'But – he came and mocked me, calling you his lady wife – '

'There was even some mummery with one of his red-roved priests, and he sat me in the high seat at his side,' Allira confirmed, 'with a knife near enough my ribs that I didn't dare speak – '

'But he didn't harm you, apart from that?'

'He used neither knife not whip, if that's what you mean,' Allira said, and dropped her eyes. Before the accusing silence of the younger girl, she burst out, 'What could I have done? Edric dead, for all I knew – you, Zandru knew where – he would have killed me,' she cried out on another gust of sobs. 'You would have done the same!'

'Had you no dagger?' Melitta raged.

'He – he took it away from me,' Allira wept.

Melitta thought, *I would have used it on myself before he could make me his doxy-puppet in his high hall*. But she did not speak the words aloud. Allira had always been a fragile, gentle girl, frightened by the cry of a hawk, too timid to ride any horse but the gentlest of palfreys, so shy and home-loving that she sought neither lover nor husband. Melitta subdued her anger and her voice to gentleness. 'Well, love, no one's blaming you; our people know better and it's no one else's business; and all the smiths of Zandru can't mend a broken egg or a girl's maidenhead, so let's think what's to be done now.'

'Did they hurt you, Meli?'

'If you mean did they rape me, no; that scarface, a curse to his manhood, had no time for me, and I suppose he thought me too fine a prize for any of his men offhand – though he'll probably fling me to one of them when the time comes, if we can't stop it.' In a renewed spasm of horror, she thought of Brynat's rabble of renegades, bandits, and half-human things from far back in the Hellers. She caught Allira's thought, even the brutal protection of the bandit chief was better than that rabble's hands. Well, she couldn't blame Lira – had she had the same choice what might she have done? Not all porridge cooked is eaten, and not all brave words can be put into acts. Nevertheless, a revulsion she could not quite conceal made her loose her sister from her arms and say dispassionately, 'Edric, I think, is in the dungeons; Brynat forbade me to go there. But I think I would feel it if he were dead. You are more psychic than I; when you pull yourself together, try to reach his mind.'

'And Storn!' Allira broke out again in frenzy. 'What has he done to protect us – lying like a log, safe and guarded by his own magic, and leaving us all to *their* tender mercies!'

'What could he have done otherwise?' Melitta asked reasonably. 'He cannot hold a sword or see to use it; at least he has made sure that no one can use him for a puppet – as they are using you.' Her eyes, fierce and angry, bored into her sister; 'Has he gotten you with child yet?'

'I don't know – it could be.'

'Curse you for a whittling,' Melitta raged. 'Don't you, even now, see what it is he wants? If it were only a willing girl, why not one – or a dozen – of the maids? Listen. I have a plan, but you must use what little sense the gods gave you for a few days at least. Wash your face, robe yourself decently, try to look like the Lady of Storn, not some camp follower torn from the kennel! Brynat thinks he has you tamed and well-married, but he is a ruffian and you

25

are a lady; you have the blood of the Seven Domains; you can outwit him if you try. Play for time, Allira! Have the vapors, play at mourning, put him off with promises – at worst, tell him that the day you know you are pregnant you will throw yourself from the battlements – and *make him believe it!* He daren't kill you, Allira; he needs you robed and jewelled in the high seat beside him, at least until he can be sure no follower or enemy will try to topple him from this height. Put him off for a few days, no more, and then – '

'Can you waken Storn to help us?' Allira gasped.

'By all the gods, what an idiot you are! Storn in trance is all that keeps us safe, Lira, and gives us time. Storn roused and in his hands – that devil's whelp would stick a knife in Edric's guts, toss me to his soldiers for a few hours' sport while I lived, and who knows if he'd even want a child from you? No, Lira, pray Storn keeps safe in trance till I can think of a plan! You do your part, keep up your courage, and I'll do mine.'

In her heart a small desperate plan was maturing. She dared not tell Allira. They might be overheard, or, if she formulated it in words, there might be among Brynat's rabble, some half-human telepath who would win favor from his outlaw lord by bearing tales of the plot. But a seed of hope had been born in her.

'Come, Allira, let us dress you as befits the Lady of Storn, and bedazzle that ruffian into respect,' she said, and prepared, again, to face Brynat without revealing any-thing.

Barron had been in the service of the Terran Empire since he was a lad in his late teens and he had served on three planets before coming to Darkover. He discovered that afternoon that he had never left Terra. He found it out by leaving it for the first time.

At the designated gate from the Terran Zone, a bored young clerk looked him over as he examined the slip from Transportation and Personnel, which stated that Barron, Class Two, was being released on liaison assignment beyond the Zone. He remarked, 'So you're the fellow who's going back into the mountains? You'd better get rid of those clothes and pick up some sort of suitable outfit for travelling here. Those togs you're wearing might do for the Zone, but back in the hills you'll get frozen – or maybe lynched. Didn't they tell you?'

They hadn't told him anything. Barron felt nonplussed; was he expected to go native? He was a Terran Empire liaison man, not a secret agent. But the clerk was the first person since the accident who had treated him like a human being, and he was grateful. 'I thought I was going as an official representative. No safe-conducts, then?'

The clerk shrugged. 'Who'd give it? You ought to be planet-wise after five years here. Terrans, or any Empire men, aren't popular outside Trade City. Or didn't you bother reading Official Directive Number Two?'

'Not the fine print.' He knew that it made it illegal, on penalty of instant deportation, for Empire men to enter, without permits, any portion of the planet outside the designated trade zones. Barron had never wanted to, and so it never entered his head to wonder why. An alien 'planet was an alien planet – there were thousands of them – and his work had always been inside the Zone.

But it was no longer.

The clerk was feeling talkative. 'Almost all the Terrans in Mapping and Exploring or the other liaison jobs wear Darkovan clothes. Warmer, and you don't collect a crowd that way. Didn't anybody tell you?'

Barron shook his head stubbornly. He didn't remind the clerk that nobody had been telling him anything for some days. In any case, he was feeling stubborn. He was doing his proper work for the Empire – he was officially appointed to it – and the Darkovans were not to tell him how to dress or act. If the Darkovans didn't like the clothes he was wearing, they could start learning the tolerance for alien customs which was the first thing required of every man who accepted work for the Terran Empire. He was satisfied with his light, warm synthetic tunic and breeches, his soft, low-cut sandals, and his short lined overcoat, which kept out the wind. Many Darkovans had adopted them in Trade City; the clothing was comfortable and indestructible. Why change it? He said a little stiffly, 'It isn't as if I were wearing Spaceforce uniform. I can see where that might be a breach of good taste. But these?'

The clerk shrugged enigmatically. 'It's your funeral,' he said. 'Here, I imagine this is your transport coming now.'

Barron looked down the roughly cobbled street, but saw no sign of any vehicle approaching. There were the usual crew of loungers, women in heavy shawls going about their business, and three men leading horses. He started to say 'where' and then realized that the three men, who were coming straight toward the gate, were leading *four* horses.

He swallowed hard. He had known in a general way that the Darkovans had small technology and used no motor transit. They used various pack and draft animals, indigenous relatives of the buffalo and the larger deer, and horses – probably descended from a strain imported from Nova Terra about a hundred years ago – for riding. It made sense. The Darkovan terrain was unsuited to road-building on a large scale, the population didn't care about it and in any case there were none of the massive mining and manufacturing operations which are necessary for surface transit. Barron, safely inside the Zone, had noticed all this and his reaction had been 'So what?' He hadn't really cared how the Darkovans lived; it had nothing to do with him. His world was spaceport dispatch: spaceships, cargo, passenger transit – Darkover was a major pivot on long-distance hypertravel because it was situated conveniently between the High Arm and Low Arm of the Galaxy – mapping ships, and the various tractors and surface machinery for servicing all of those. He was not prepared for the change from spaceship to pack animals.

The three men paused, letting go the reins of the horses, which were well-trained and stood quietly. The foremost of the three men, a sturdy young man in his twenties, said, 'You are the Terran representative Daniel Firth Barron?' He had some trouble with the name.

'*Z'par servu.*' The polite Darkovan phrase, *at your service*, brought a faint agreeable smile from the young man as he replied in some formula Barron couldn't understand and then shifted back to Trade City language, saying, 'I am Colryn. This is Lerrys, and this, Gwynn. Are you ready? Can you leave at once? Where are your baggages?'

'I'm ready when you are.' Barron indicated the duffel bag, which held his few possessions, and the large but light case which held the equipment he must use. 'The bag can be knocked around as much as you like; it's only clothes. But be careful not to drop the crate; it's breakable.'

'Gwynn, you see to that,' Colryn said. 'We have pack animals waiting outside the city, but for the moment we can carry them with us. It isn't easy to manage pack animals on the streets here, as narrow as they are.'

Barron realized that they were waiting for him to mount. He reminded himself that this assignment was all that stood between him and ruin, but that didn't seem very important at the moment. He wanted, for the first time in his adult life, to run. He set his mouth hard and said very stiffly. 'I should warn you, I've never been on a horse in my life.'

'I am sorry,' Colryn said. His politeness was almost excessive. 'There is no other way to go where we are going.'

The one introduced as Lerrys swung Barron's duffel bag up to his saddle. He said, 'I'll take this, you'll have enough trouble with your reins, then.' His Terran was substantially better than Colryn's, being virtually accentless. 'You'll soon pick up riding; I did. Colryn, why don't you show him how to mount? And ride beside him until he gets over being nervous.'

Nervous! Barron felt like snarling at the youngster that he had been facing strange worlds when this boy was playing with his toys, then he relaxed. *What the hell, I am nervous, the kid would have to be blind not to see it.*

Before he realized how it had happened, he was in the saddle, his feet slipped through the high ornate stirrups, moving slowly down the street and away from the Terran Zone. He was too confused and too busy keeping his balance to give it a single backward look.

He had never been at close quarters with Darkovans before. At the restaurants and shops in Trade City, they had been dark impassive faces serving him and strangers at a safe distance to be ignored. Now he was among them for an indefinite period of time, with only the most casual of warnings, the dimmest of preparations.

This never happened in the Terran Empire! Damn it, you were never supposed to be assigned work outside your speciality; then if they actually sent you into the field on a strange planet, you were supposed to get all sorts of briefing and training! At the moment it was taking all the concentration he could muster to stay on his horse.

It was the better part of an hour before he began to relax, to feel that a fall was less imminent, and to spare a few minutes to look at his three companions.

All three were younger than Barron, as well as he could

judge. Colryn was tall, lanky yet delicately built, and his face was narrow and fine, with a shadow of brown curly beard. His voice was soft, but he seemed unusually self-possessed for so young a man, and he talked and laughed with animation as they rode. Lerrys was sturdy, with hair almost red enough for a Terran, and seemed hardly into his twenties. Gwynn, the third, was swart and tall, the oldest of the three; except for a nod and brief greeting, he had paid no attention to Barron and seemed a little aloof from the younger men.

All three wore loose heavy breeches, falling in flaps over high, carefully-fitted boots, and laced tunic-like shirts in rich, dark colors, Gwynn and Colryn had thick, fur-lined riding cloaks, and Lerrys a short loose fur jacket with a hood. All three wore short gauntlets, knives in their belts and smaller knives in pockets at the top of their boots; Gwynn had a sword as well, although for riding it was swung across the crupper of his horse. They all had hair cut smoothly below their ears and a variety of amulets of jewelry. They looked fierce, bright and barbaric. Barron, aware of his own thoroughly civilized clothing, hair, grooming and manner, felt queerly frightened. *Damn it, I'm not ready for this sort of thing!*

They rode at first through cobbled streets, between the crowded houses and markets of the Old Town; then along wider stone roads where the going was smoother, between high houses set back behind gardens and unfamiliar high towers. Finally the stone road ended to become trampled grass and the riders turned aside toward a long, low enclosure and through wooden and stone fences and gateways into a sort of compound of reddish, trampled earth, where several dozen unfamiliarly dressed men were doing various things; loading and unloading animals, saddling and grooming them, cooking over open fires or on braziers, washing and splashing in a wooden trough, and carrying buckets of feed and water to the beasts. It was very cold and very confusing, and Barron was glad, at last, to reach the lee of a rough stone wall, where he was permitted to slide from his horse and turn it over, at Colryn's nod, to a roughly dressed man who came to lead it away.

He walked between Gwynn and Lerrys, Colryn remaining behind to see to the animals, under a shelter roofed and walled against the wind. Lerrys said, 'You're not used to riding; why don't you rest while we get food ready? And haven't you any riding clothes? I can bring your bag – it would be better to change into them now.'

Although Barron knew that the youngster was trying to be kind, he felt irritated at the continued harping on this point. 'The clothes I have with me are just like this; I'm sorry.'

'In that case you'd better come with me,' Lerrys said, and led him out of the shelter again, through the opposite end of the long enclosure. Heads turned to follow them as they passed; someone shouted something and people laughed loudly. He heard repeated murmurs of *Terranan*, which didn't need any interpreting. Lerrys turned and said firmly, '*Chaireth.*' That caused a momentary silence and then a brief flurry of quiet words and mutters. They all moved away with some deference as the young redhead motioned to them. Finally the two came out into a market or shop – mostly clay jars and coarse glassware, a multitude of loose garments lying over baskets and barrels. Lerrys said firmly, 'You can't possibly travel into the mountains in the outfit you're wearing. I don't mean to sound offensive, but it's impossible.'

'I wasn't given any orders –'

'Listen, my friend' – Lerrys used the Darkovan word *com'ii* – 'You have no idea how cold it gets, travelling in the open, especially back in the hills. Your clothes may be warm' – he touched a fold of the light synthetic – 'but only for conditions between walls. The Hellers are the very bones of the earth. Your feet will be sore, riding in those things, not to mention –'

Barron, now fiercely embarrassed, had to say flatly, 'I can't afford it.'

Lerrys drew a deep breath. 'My foster father has ordered

me to provide everything that is necessary for your well-being, Mr Barron.' Barron was surprised at the manner of address – the Darkovans did not use honorifics or surnames – but then, Lerrys apparently spoke excellent Terran. He wondered if the young man were a professional interpreter. 'Who is your foster father?'

'Valdir Alton of the Comyn Council,' Lerrys said briefly. Even Barron had heard of the Comyn – the hereditary caste of Darkovan rulers – and it silenced him. If the Comyn had anything to do with this and wanted him to wear Darkovan clothes, there was no use arguing.

After a brief period of spirited bargaining of which Barron – who knew considerable of the Darkovan language, more because he was quick and fluent at languages, than because he had been interested – could follow very little, Lerrys said, 'I hope these will meet with your approval. I knew you would not care to wear bright colors; I do not myself.' He handed Barron a pile of clothing, mostly in dark fabrics that looked like linen, with a heavy fur jacket like the one he himself was wearing. 'It's hard to manage a cloak, riding, unless you grew up wearing one.' There was also a pair of high boots.

'Better try the boots for fit,' he suggested.

Barron bent and slipped off his sandals. The clothing seller chuckled and said something Barron couldn't follow about sandals and Lerrys said fiercely, 'The *Chaireth* is Lord Alton's guest!' The merchant gulped, muttered some phrases of apology and fell silent. The boots fitted as if they had been made for him, and though they felt strange along his ankles and calves, Barron had to admit they were comfortable. Lerrys picked up the sandals and stuck them in Barron's pocket. 'You could wear them indoors, I suppose.'

Barron would have answered, but before the words reached his lips a curious dizziness swept over him.

He was standing in a great, vaulted hall, lighted only by a few flickering torches. Below him he could hear the shouts of drunken men; and he could smell torches, roasting

33

meat, and an odd acrid odor that confused him and made him feel sick. He grasped at a ring in the wall, found that it was not there; the wall was not there. He was back in the blowing wind and cloudy sunlight of the fenced compound, his pile of clothing fallen to the grass at his feet, and young Lerrys staring up at him, shaken and puzzled.

'Are you all right, Barron? You looked – a bit odd.'

Barron nodded, glad to conceal his face by stooping to gather up his clothing. He was relieved when Lerrys left him in the shelter and he could sink down on the rough floor and lean against the wall, shuddering.

That again! Was he going mad? If it had been due to the stress of his job, now that he had been removed from the dispatch board it should have stopped. Yet, although brief, this time had been more vivid than the others. Shivering, he shut his eyes and tried not to think until Colryn, coming to the edge of the open wall of the shelter, called to him.

Two or three men in rough, dark clothing were moving around the fire; Colryn did not introduce them. Barron, in response to gestures, joined Gwynn and Lerrys at the trough where men were washing. It was growing dusky and the icy evening wind was coming up, but they all washed long and thoroughly. Barron was shivering uncontrollably and thinking with some longing of the Darkovan fur jacket, but he took his turn and washed face and hands more than he'd normally have done; he didn't want them to think Terrans were dirty – and in any case riding had left him dirtier than pushing buttons and watching circuit relays. The water was bitterly cold, and he shook with the chill, his face bitten by the bitter wind.

They sat around the fire out of the wind, and after murmuring a brief formula, Gwynn began handing food around. Barron accepted the plate he was given, which held some sweet boiled grain covered with a splash of acrid sauce, a large lump of meat and a small bowl of thick bittersweet stuff vaguely like chocolate. It was all good, although it was hard to manage the tough meat which the others sliced into paper-thin slices with the knives in their belts; it had been salted and dried in some manner and was almost like leather. Barron pulled a pack of cigarettes from his pockets and lighted one, drawing the smoke gratefully into his mouth; it tasted ambrosial.

Gwynn scowled at him and said in an undertone to Colryn, 'First the sandals and now this – ' looking with direct rudeness at Barron, he asked a question of which Barron could make out only the unfamiliar word *embredin*. Lerrys raised his head from his plate, saw Barron's cigarette and shook his head slightly, then said '*Chaireth*' again, rather deprecatingly, to Gwynn and got up to drop down beside Barron.

'I wouldn't smoke here if I were you,' he said. 'I know it is your custom, but it is offensive among the men of the Domains.'

'What was he saying?'

Lerrys flushed. 'He was asking, to put it in the simplest possible terms, if you were an – an effeminate. It was partly those damned sandals of yours, and partly – well, as I say, men do not smoke here. It is reserved for women.'

With an irritable gesture Barron ground out his cigarette. This was going to be worse than he thought. 'What's that word you used – chaireth?'

'Stranger,' Lerrys said. Barron picked up a lump of meat again, and Lerrys said, almost apologizing, 'I should have provided you with a knife.'

'No matter,' Barron said, 'I wouldn't know how to use it anyway.'

'Nevertheless – ' Lerrys began again, but Barron did not hear him. The fire before them slid away – or rather, flared up, and in the midst of the flames, tall, bluish, and glowing, he saw –

A woman.

A woman again, standing in the midst of flames. He thought he cried out in the moment before the figure changed, grew and was, again, the great chained Being, regal, burning, searing her beauty into his heart and brain. Barron gripped his hands until the nails bit into the palms.

The apparition was gone.

Lerrys was staring at him, white and shaken. 'Sharra,' he breathed, 'Sharra, the golden-chained –'

Barron reached out and grabbed him. He said, hoarsely, disregarding the men at the fire, which was once again the tiny, cooking fire, 'You saw it? *You* saw it?'

Lerrys nodded without speaking. His face was so white that small freckles stood out. He said at last with a gasp, 'Yes, I saw. What I can't understand is – how *you* saw! What in the Devil's name are you?'

Barron, almost too shaken to speak, said, 'I don't know. That keeps happening. I have no idea why. I'd like to know why you can see it, too.'

Struggling for composure, Lerrys said, 'What you saw – it is a Darkovan archetype, a Goddess form. I don't completely understand. I know that many Terrans have some telepathic power. Someone must be broadcasting these images and somehow you have the power to pick them up. I – ' He hesitated. 'I must speak to my foster father before I tell you more.' He fell silent, then said with sudden resolution; 'Tell me, what would you rather be called?'

'Dan will do,' Barron said.

'Dan then. You are going to have trouble in the mountains; I thought you would be an ordinary Terran, and not aware – ' He stopped, biting his lip. 'I am under a pledge,' he said at last, 'and I cannot break it even for this. But you are going to have trouble and you will need a friend. Do you know why no one would lend you a knife?'

Barron shook his head. 'Never occurred to me to ask. Like I said, I can't use one anyway.'

'You are a Terran,' Lerrys said. 'By custom and law here – a knife or any other weapon must never be lent or given, except between sworn friends or kinfolk. To say "my knife is yours" is a pledge. It means that you will defend the other – therefore, a knife or any weapon, must be bought, or captured in battle, or made for you. Yet,' he said, with a sudden laugh, 'I will give you this – and I have my reasons.' He stooped down and drew a small sharp knife from the pocket in his boot. 'It is yours,' he said, suddenly very serious. 'I mean what I say, Barron. Take it from me, and say "yours and mine" '.

Barron, feeling embarrassed and strange, fumbled at the hilt of the small blade. 'Mine, then, and yours. Thank you, Lerrys.' The intensity of the moment caught him briefly up into it, and he found himself staring into the younger man's eyes almost as if words passed between them.

The other men around the fire were staring at them, Gwynn frowning in surprised disapproval, Colryn looking puzzled, and vaguely – Barron wondered how he knew – jealous.

Barron fell to his food, both puzzled and relieved. It was easier to eat with the knife in his hand; later he found it fitted easily into the little pocket at the top of his boot. Lerrys did not speak to him again, but he grinned briefly at Barron now and then, and Barron knew that, for some reason, the young man had adopted him as a friend. It was a strange feeling. He was not a man to make friends easily – he had no close ones – and now a young man from a strange world, guessing at his confusion, had thrust unexpected friendship on him. He wondered why and what would happen next.

He shrugged, finished his meal, and followed Colryn's gestured directions – to rinse his plate and bowl and pack them with the others and to help with the spreading of blankets inside the shelter. It was very dark now; cold rain began to spray across the compound; and he was glad to be inside. There was, he realized, a subtle difference in the way they treated him now; he wondered why, and though he told himself it made no difference, he was glad of it.

Once in the night, wrapped in fur blankets, surrounded by sleeping men, he woke to stare at nothingness and feel his body gripped with weightlessness and cold winds again. Lerrys, sleeping a few feet away, stirred and murmured, and the sound brought Barron back to the moment.

It was going to be one hell of a trip if this keeps on happening every few hours.

And there wasn't a thing he could do about it.

—— 4 ——

A voice called in Melitta's dreams.

'Melitta! Melitta, sister, *breda*, wake! Listen to me!'

She sat up in the dark, desperately grasping at the voice. 'Storn,' she gasped, half aloud, 'is it you?'

'I can speak to you only a little while like this, *breda*, so listen. You are the only one who can help me. Allira cannot hear, and in any case she is too frail and timid, she would die in the hills. Edric is wounded and prisoned. It must be you, little one. Dare you help me?'

'Anything,' she whispered, her heart pounding. Her eyes groped at the dark. 'Are you here? Can we escape? Shall I make a light?'

'Hush. I am not here; I speak to your mind only. I have tried to waken hearing in you for these last four days and at last you hear me. Listen, sister – you must go alone. You are only lightly guarded; you can shake them off. But you must go now, before snow closes the passes. I have found someone to help you. I will send him to you at Carthon.'

'Where . . .'

'At Carthon,' the fading voice whispered and was silent. Melitta whispered aloud, 'Storn, Storn, don't go,' but the voice had failed and faded into exhaustion. She was alone in the darkness, her brother's voice still ringing like an echo in her ears.

Carthon – but where was Carthon? Melitta had never been more than a few miles from her home; she had never been beyond the mountains and her ideas of geography were hazy. Carthon might be over the next ridge, or it might be at the world's end.

She flung agonized queries into the darkness. *How can I,*

where shall I go? but there was no answer, only darkness and silence. Had it been a dream born of her frenzy to escape, or had her brother in his magical trance, somehow managed to reach her mind in truth? If it were so, then she could do nothing but obey.

Melitta of Storn was a mountain girl with all that implied. The prime root of her being was the clan loyalty to Storn, not only as her elder brother, but as the head of his house. That he was blind and incapacitated, that he could not have defended her and her sister and younger brother – not to mention their people – in this crisis, made no difference. She did not censure him even in her thoughts and believed, when Allira did so, that the girl's sufferings at Brynat's hands had turned her brain. Now he had laid the task on her to escape and find help, and it never occurred to her not to obey.

She rose from her bed, pulled a fur robe around her shoulders – for the night was bitterly cold and the stone floors had never known fire – and thrust her feet into furry socks, then, moving surely in the dark, found flints and tinder and struck a small lamp – so small that the light was not much bigger than the head of a pin. She sat down before the light, cheered a little by the tiny flame, and began to plan what she could do.

She knew already what she must do – escape from the castle before snow closed the passes, and somehow make her way to Carthon, where her brother would send someone to help her. But how this could be accomplished, she found it hard to imagine.

Guards still followed her at a respectful distance, everywhere she went through the halls. Dark and late though it was, she was sure that even if she left her room they would rouse from where they slept and follow. They feared Brynat more than they longed for sleep. Their fear of him was made clear to her when she realized that not one of them had ventured to lay a hand on her. She wondered if she should be grateful for this, and thrust the thought aside. That was to fall into his trap.

Like all mountain girls, Melitta was enough of a realist

to think the next logical step: could she seduce one of the guards into letting her escape? She thought it unlikely. They feared Brynat, and he had ordered them to let her alone. More likely the guard would accept her advances, take what she offered, then go directly to Brynat with the story and win approval of his chief as well. After which, Brynat might well punish her by turning her over to the outlaws for a plaything. That was a blind alley – she could have made herself do it, but it would probably be no use.

She went to the window, pulling her furs closer about her, and leaned out. *You must be gone before the snow closes the passes.* She was a mountain girl, with weather and storms in her blood. It seemed to Melitta that she could almost smell from afar, borne on the chill night wind, the smell of far-off clouds pregnant with snow.

The night was not far advanced. Idriel and Liriel swung in the sky; Mormalor, faint and pearly, hung half-shadowed on the shoulder of the mountain. If she could manage somehow to leave the castle before dawn . . .

She could not go now. Brynat's men were still at their nightly drinking party in the great hall; Allira might send for her still, and she dared not be found absent. But in the hours between deep night and dawn, when even the air was sluggish, she might devise a plan, and be far away before mid-morning discovered that she was not in her room. She closed the window, cuddling herself in the furs, and went back to make plans.

Once out of the castle she wondered where she could go. It would be to Carthon, wherever that was, eventually. But she could not make Carthon in a single night; she would need shelter and food, for it might be a journey halfway to the world's end. Once clear of Castle Storn, perhaps some of her brother's vassals would shelter her. Although they were without power to protect against Brynat's attack, she knew that they loved Storn and many of them knew and loved her. They would at least let her hide among them for a day or two until the hue and cry died down; they might help provide her with food for the journey, and it might be that one of them could set her on the road to Carthon.

The nearest of the great lords were the Aldarans, of Castle Aldaran near High Kimbi; they had, as far as she knew, no blood feud with Storns and no commitment to Brynat, but it seemed unlikely that they would, or could come to the aid of Storn at this time. Her grandmother's kinfolk had been Leyniers, related to the great Comyn Domain of Alton, but even the Comyn Council's writ did not run here in the mountains.

It did not occur to Melitta to censure her brother, but it did occur to her that, knowing himself weak, he might well have attempted to place himself under the protection of one of the powerful mountain lords. But always before, the chasms and crags surrounding Storn had made them impregnable; and – a Storn swear fealty to another house? Never!

He could have married Allira – or me – to some son of a great house. Then we would have blood kin to protect us – bare is the back with no brother to guard it!

Well, he had not, and the time for fretting was long past – *chickens can't be put back into eggs!* The evil bird that had hatched from this oversight was out and flying, and only Melitta had the freedom and the strength to save something from the wreck.

Carrying the tiny lamp, she went to her chests. She could not go in long skirts and mantles. At the bottom of her chest was an old riding cloak, woven of thick heavy fabric from the valley and lined with fur; it was not rich enough to rouse greed to anyone she passed but it was warm and durable. There was an old shabby pair of her brother's riding breeches, patched with leather, which she had worn for riding about the estate; it was a wiser choice than her own long, loose riding mantle. She added a knitted blouse, a long, thick, lined tunic, socks knitted from the spun fur of the forge folk, and her fur boots. She made a small parcel of a change of linen and some small trinkets, which she might sell or barter for help on the way. Finally she braided her hair and tied it into a woolen cap. This done, she put out the lamp and went to the balcony again. Until this moment, the actual preparation for the journey had obscured the really basic fact: exactly *how* was she to get out of the castle?

There were secret passages. She knew some of them. There was one, for instance, leading from the wine cellars near the old dungeon. The only thing necessary was to get into the wine cellar so that she could get into the secret passage. Perfectly simple. And what would her guards be doing while she descended the stairs and went into the wine cellar, conveniently managing to leave them outside? Drinking wine? That might be fine, if she could get them drunk enough, but they would certainly be suspicious at anything she offered them, on guard for a trick.

Another exit from the castle – calling it secret was a mere technicality, a way of saying that it had been unused for years and nobody bothered guarding it any more – was the passageway that led down into the cliffs and the abandoned forges where, in an earlier day of Darkover, the dark, stunted mountain people had worshipped the fires that lit their forges. There they had made the ancient swords and the strangely propertied artifacts which those who had never seen them used, called magical. The fires and forges had been silent for centuries, the little people withdrawn into the deeper hills; the Storns had come long after they were gone. As a child Melitta, with her brothers and sister, had explored the caves and abandoned dwellings of the forge folk. But they and all their magic were gone. Their poor and scattered remnants now dwelt in villages near Storn, and they had been captured and driven along with the farm folk; they were more helpless than Melitta herself.

She looked over the balcony again, her mouth curving in what might have been a smile in better days. *I need wings,* she thought. *My guards are too much afraid of Brynat to molest me here; while I stay in this room, they will stay outside in that hallway, and swear to him that I am inside here. I should have managed these things better; I should have spent my child-*

hood in a room with one of the secret passages. I can think of a dozen ways to get out of the castle – but I have to get out of this room first, and I can't think of a way to do that.

A faint glimmer of light wavering beneath her showed her that, on the lower floor and some rooms away, Allira moved in the Royal Suite. She thought, despairingly, *Storn should have wakened Allira. There is the old hidden way from the Royal Suite, down into the cliff people's village. Allira could simply wait till Brynat was sleeping, and slip away . . .*

Mad schemes spun in her mind. She had access to her sister; the guards would follow her to the doors of the Royal Suite but not follow her inside; could she manage to get in there and find the old entrance to the passage? At what hour could they be safe from Brynat's intrusion? Could she count on Allira to trick him, drug him, even hold him in talk or in sensual play while she, Melitta, slipped past?

I dare not depend on Allira, she thought with something like despair. *She would not betray me, but she would not have courage to help me, or risk angering Brynat, either.*

If I went down to her rooms, with the guards following me – how long could I count on being alone with her before they summoned Brynat, or grew suspicious when I did not return? And if I vanished from her rooms – they would tear her to pieces, to find out what way I had gone, and I would be pursued before the sun was well up. That's no help.

But the thought persisted. It might very well be her only chance. It was, of course, to risk everything on one throw; if Brynat returned while she was with Allira, something might rouse his suspicions and she would be consigned to securer custody. For all she knew, her guards had orders to report to Brynat if she and her sister spoke together for more than a few minutes.

But if no one knew I was with Allira?

How could she get to Allira's room unseen?

The old Darkovans had mastered the secret of such things. The magic electrical net which protected Storn's trance was only one of the powers with which Melitta was familiar – but none of them were of use to her now. There

43

were magical cloaks which threw a veil of illusion around the wearer and let them walk unseen, by bending the light, but if Storn had ever owned one, Melitta did not know where it was, or how to use it. She could slip up to the Sunrise Tower, if she could get there, and pull the magical bird plumage over her head, and fly out and away from the castle – but only in illusion. What she saw would be real enough – Storn, she knew, had watched the battle that way – but her body would lie in trance in the Tower, and sooner or later, she would be drawn back to it. That was not the kind of escape which would do any good. *I need wings,* she thought again. *If I could fly right off this balcony and down into that same Royal Suite where Brynat has taken Allira . . .*

She stopped in mid-thought, grimly. She had no wings. Thinking about them was no good. But she had two sturdy arms, two sturdy legs, ten strong fingers and she had been trained since childhood in rock climbing.

She went to the edge of the balcony, fantasies and plans vanishing in a cold, realistic assessment of the problem. She could not fly down to the Royal Suite. But, with strength, caution, and good luck, it was remotely possible that she could *climb* down to it.

She leaned over, fighting a sudden surge of dizziness. A hundred feet of rough, sheared stone fell away into a chasm below. But the castle wall was not sheer, not smooth. Centuries ago, it had been built of rough stone, the very bones of the mountain, hewn in great lumps and cemented into place with ancient tools which would have blunted too swiftly if the stone had had to be smoothed. A wealth of window ledges, archer's slits, balconies, outside stairways and projections lumped and ridged the gray sides of the old castle.

When I was a child, she thought, *Storn and I used to climb everywhere. I was whipped once for frightening our nurse out of her senses by climbing to a third-level balcony and making faces at her from the arbor. I taught Edric to climb on the balconies down lower. I've never climbed this high – I was afraid of falling. But this part of the castle should be as climbable as the lower part.*

44

She knew that if she fell she would be broken on the crags far below. *But why should I fall from two hundred feet in the air, if I could manage not to fall from fifteen feet?*

You never thought about that because it wouldn't have mattered if you did fall from fifteen feet, her common sense told her, but she hushed the voice, packed up the thought into a tiny box, shoved it into the back of her mind and left it there. *And suppose I do get killed,* she told herself defiantly. *Edric didn't mind risking being killed in the siege, or if he did mind, he risked it anyway. I took bow and arrow myself, and I could have been shot or knifed down on the ramparts. If I was willing to die then, in the hope of defending Storn Heights, then why should I hesitate to take the same sort of risk now? If I get killed, I get killed, and at least I won't have to worry about Brynat's rabble lining up to take turns raping me.*

It wasn't exactly a comforting thought, but she decided that she could make it do for the moment. She hesitated only a moment, her hands on the railing. Off went the fur-lined gloves; she thrust them deep into the pockets of Edric's breeches. She buttoned the cloak back and tied it into the smallest possible compass at her waist, hoping it would not catch on a projection of stone. Finally she slipped off her boots, standing shivering on the stone balcony, and tied them together by their laces round her neck. If the thongs caught on a stone she might strangle, but without boots she would be helpless in the snow, and her trained weather sense told her that the snow could not be very long delayed. Then, without giving herself time to think she swung herself up and over the edge of the balcony, sat there for a moment taking the exact bearings of the room and balcony she wanted – forty feet below her and almost a hundred feet away to the left – and slipped down, lodging her stockinged feet in a crevice of the stone, finding a handhold to spread-eagle herself against the rough wall.

The crevices between the stone seemed smaller than when she had climbed about on them as a child, and she had to move by feel on the cold stone. Her feet ached with the cold before she had moved five yards, and she felt first one, then another of her nails split back and break as she clutched the dark, rough stone. The moonlight was pale and fitful, and twice a white streak that she took for a crevice in the paleness turned out to be a crumbling, evil-smelling bird-dropping. But Melitta clung like a limpet to each crevice, never moving more than one hand or one foot until she was securely anchored in some new hold.

Evanda be praised, she thought grimly, *that I'm strong and tough from riding! If I were a girl to sit over my sewing, I'd drop off in two yards!* Even strong as she was, she felt every muscle trembling with cold and tension. She felt, also, that in the pale moonlight, she must be clearly visible against the side of the castle, a target for an arrow from any sentry who happened to look up on his rounds. Once she froze, whimpering as a small light and a fragment of voice, blown on the wind, came round the corner, and she knew one of Brynat's soldiers on some business below passed beneath her. Melitta shut her eyes and prayed he would not look up. He did not; he went on singing drunkenly and, almost exactly beneath her, a hundred feet below, and on the narrow path between the castle and the cliffs, opened the fly of his breeches and urinated into the abyss. She held herself taut, trembling against hysterical laughter. After what seemed an hour he stooped, picked up his lantern, shrugged his clothes in place and stumbled on his way again. Melitta thought she had forgotten how to breathe, but she managed it again, and forced her taut fingers, gripping at a stone, to move again toward the lighted balcony below.

Inch by slow inch – a finger, a toe, a cold yard at a time – the girl crept like an ant down the wall. Once, her heart flipped over and stopped as a pebble encrusted in cement broke away under her fingers, and she heard it slide away and ricochet off a projection beneath her, rebound with what sounded like gunfire off the rocks below, and finally clatter into the darkness. Every muscle tight, she held her breath for minutes, sure that the sound would bring soldiers running, but when she opened her eyes again, the castle still lay bathed in the empty light of the setting moons and she still clung to the wall in her comforting solitude.

The moonlight had dimmed considerably past the shoulder of the mountains, and thick mists were beginning to rise below, when at last her feet touched the stone of the balcony and she let go and slid, dropped down on the stone railing, and crouched there, just breathing in deep gasps of relief. When she could move again, she slipped her hands into her gloves, her feet into the fur-lined boots, and wrapped herself tightly in the cloak, grabbing it tight to lessen her shivering.

The first hurdle was passed. But now she must get inside and attract Allira's attention without running the risk that Brynat would see. She had come too far to be stopped now!

She crept like a small shaking ghost across the stone balcony and pressed her face against the veined colored glass, joined with strips of metal, which closed the double doors of the balcony. The doors were bolted inside and lined with heavy thick curtains of tapestry, and Melitta had a sudden hysterical picture of herself perched out there like a bird for days, uselessly rapping like a bird at the glass, unheard, until somebody looked up and saw her there.

She also feared that it might be Brynat who drew aside those curtains and looked straight out into her eyes.

She tried to force herself to approach the window, but the picture of Brynat's fierce face was so compelling that she literally could not make herself raise her hand. She *knew* he was behind that tapestry. She sank down, nerveless and shaking, and waited, her mind spinning.

Storn, Storn, you came to me before, help me now! Brother, brother! Gods of the mountains, what shall I do? She begged and commanded her weak limbs to move, but she kept on crouching there, frozen and motionless, for what seemed like hours. Finally, slowly, her frozen body and brain began to work again, and she began to think.

When we were children, Allira and I could reach one another's minds like this. Not always and not often, but if one of us was in danger the other would know; when the wild bird pack had her cut off on the island, I knew and I brought help. She was fourteen then, and I was only eight. I cannot have lost the power, or Storn could not have reached me tonight. But if all my mind is giving off is fear, Allira wouldn't know if she did hear me; she'd think it was just part of her own panic.

She had had almost no training. Storn, being blind and thus debarred from the usual pursuits of men of his caste, had explored the old telepathic ways. But to his brother and sisters, these had been dreams, fantasies, games and tricks – pleasant perhaps for pastime, but not worthy of serious study. There was too much else that was real and present and necessary to the moment. Melitta spent a moment berating herself for not spending more time with Storn learning about the old speech of mind to mind, but common sense came to her rescue. She reminded herself of the old proverb. *Foresight could make wise men of Durraman's donkeys!* She might as well blame herself for Allira's not having been married to a strong husband with eighty fighting men to defend them.

She put her hand out to rap on the glass sharply, and again the clear picture of Brynat looking out into the storm came to her; it was so instant and compelling that she physically shrank back and pressed herself against the railing, folding herself up into her cloak. It was just in time; a browned hand drew the tapestry aside, and Brynat's scarred visage turned from side to side, trying to penetrate the darkness.

Melitta shrank against the railing and tried to make herself invisible. After a minute that seemed endless, Brynat turned away and the lamp went out. The tapestry dropped back into place. Melitta dropped, gasping, to the stones, and lay there trying not to breathe.

Time dragged. The moon set, and the shivering girl grew colder and colder. After hours, so long that she began to wonder if the sun would come up and find her there, a thin fine rain began to fall, and this spurred her; she realized that whatever she risked, she must be gone by sunrise; she much be somewhere that she could lie hidden by day. Even if she must chip the glass of the doors and cut Brynat's throat while he slept, she must make some move!

As she poised her muscles for action, a faint light glimmered again between the tapestries. Melitta gathered herself to spring against the bolts; then a fine hand moved through the gap, the bolt shuddered in the wood and her sister Allira, wrapped in a long woolen shift, her hair disheveled, thrust the door outward and, her eyes great and staring, looked straight into Melitta's face.

Melitta raised a hand to her mouth, frightened of Allira's nerves and a sudden outcry, but Allira only clasped her hands to her heart with a gasp of relief. She whispered, '*I knew* you were there, and I couldn't believe – Melitta, how did you come here?'

Melitta replied only with a jerk of her head toward the rocks and a whispered 'No time now! Brynat – '

'Asleep,' Allira said laconically, 'He sleeps with one eye, like a cat, but just now – never mind that. Melitta – are you armed?'

'Not with a weapon I could kill him with, without outcry,' Melitta said flatly. 'And you'd still have his men to deal with, and they would be worse.' Watching Allira flinch, she knew that her sister had already considered and rejected that escape.

'The secret passage through the old cliff-town; have any of Brynat's men discovered it?'

'No – Melitta, you cannot go that way; you'll be lost in the caves, you'd die in the mountains if you ever found your way out – and where would you go?'

'Carthon,' Melitta said briefly, 'wherever that is. I don't suppose you know?'

'I know only that it's a city beyond the passes, which was great in the days of the Seven Domains. Melitta, are you really going to dare this?'

'It's this or die here,' Melitta said bluntly. 'You seem able to stand it here, though – '

'I don't want to die.'

Allira was almost sobbing and Melitta hushed her

roughly. It was not Allira's fault that she was so timid. Perhaps even such protection as Brynat could give seemed better than a desperate trek through strange crags, passes and mountains. *Maybe I ought to be like that too*, Melitta thought, *maybe that's a woman's proper attitude, but I suppose there's something wrong with me – and I'm glad. I'd rather die taking the chance of doing something to help Storn.*

But the brief moment of censure for her sister passed. After all, Allira had already faced, or so it seemed to Allira herself, the worst that could happen to her; what more had she to fear? By escaping now, she would only lose the life she had saved at such cost.

'You must go, then, before sunrise,' Allira said with quick resolution. 'Quick, while Brynat sleeps and before the guards come in' – a brief flicker of something like her old smile – 'as they do each night, to make sure I have not killed him while he sleeps.'

The wind blew briefly into the room and was barred out again as the two girls slipped inside. Brynat sprawled and ugly in the great bed, breathing stertorously. After one blazing look of hate, Melitta averted her eyes, creeping past him silently, holding her breath and trying not to think, as if her very hate might wake their enemy. She breathed more freely when they were in the ornate reception room of the suite, but her hands were still clenched with tension and terror.

There were the carven chests, the hangings and the strange beasts around the elaborate false fireplace. She pressed the hilt of the marble sword there and the stone slid away, revealing the old stair. She clutched Allira's hands, wanting to say something but falling silent in desperation. She went forward. Whatever happened, she was safe or dead.

Allira might somehow summon up the courage to come – but the escaping, Melitta knew with a practical grimness, was only the beginning. She had a long way to go, and she could not encumber herself with anyone who did not share her own desperate resolve; at this point, even if Allira had begged to come with her, she would have refused.

She said briefly, 'The guards outside my room think I'm still in there. Try anything you can to keep them from finding out how I've gone. You saw nothing; you heard nothing.'

Allira clutched at her, a frightened hug and kiss. 'Shall I – shall I get you Brynat's knife? He would search me for it, but when he didn't find it, he'd only think he lost it.'

Melitta nodded, a tardy spasm of admiration for her frightened sister touching her. She stood frozen, not daring to move, as Allira crept back into the bedroom, and then returned with a long, unsheathed knife, in her hand. Allira thrust it into the top of Melitta's boot. Allira had something else in her hand, wadded together in a torn linen coif. Melitta glanced hastily at the soggy mess; it was a torn half-loaf of bread, some cut slices of roast meat, and a large double handful of sticky sweets. Uncritically, she wrapped it up again and put it into her deepest pocket.

'Thank you, Lira. It will keep me going for a day or two, and if I don't find any help by then, it's no use anyhow. I must go; it will be light in three hours.' She dared not frame a goodbye in words; it would have loosened the floodgates of her fear. 'Give me your gold chain, unless you think Brynat will miss it; I can hide it in a pocket and the links will pass current, though it's not as good as a copper one would have been.'

Allira smiled a wavering smile. 'The amulet didn't protect me, did it? Maybe it will do better for you. *Lucky charms protect you only if you have your own luck.*' She pulled off the long chain, looping it twice and put it over Melitta's head. Melitta clutched at the small amulet, suddenly touched – Allira had worn it since she was three years old; it had been their mother's and grandmother's.

She said quietly, 'I'll bring it back,' gave Allira a quick kiss, and without another word, plunged into the long deep stairwell. She heard Allira sob softly, as above her the passage darkened and the light went out.

She was alone in the depths of the castle.

5

'We should reach Armida by nightfall.' Colryn drew his horse to a walk in the neck of the narrow pass, waiting for the others to draw abreast of them, and looked across at Barron with a brief smile. 'Tired of travelling?'

Barron shook his head without answering. 'Good thing, because, although the Comyn Lord may want us to break our journey there for a day or two, after that we start into the hills.'

Barron chuckled to himself. If, according to Colryn, they started into the *hills* tomorrow, he wondered what they had been travelling for these past four days. Every day since they had left the plains where the Terran Trade City lay, they had been winding down the side of one mountain and up along the side of another, till he had lost count of the peaks and slopes.

And yet he was not tired. He was hardened now to riding, and sat his horse easily; and, although he would not have known how to say so, every inch of the road had held him in a sort of spell he did not understand and could not explain.

He had expected to travel this road filled with bitterness, resentment and grim resignation – he had left behind him everything he knew: his work, such friends as he had, the whole familiar world made by the men who had spanned great giant steps across the Galaxy. He had been going into exile and strangeness.

Yet – how could he explain it even to himself? – the long road had held him almost in a dream. It had been like learning a language once known but long forgotten. He had felt the strange world reach out and grip him fast and say 'Stranger, come; you are coming home.' It gave him a sensation, of riding through a dream, or under water, with everything that happened insulated by a curtain of unreality.

Now and then, as if surfacing from a very long dive, the old self he had been, during those years when he sat at the dispatcher's board in the Terran Trade City would come to the surface and sit there blinking. He tried, once, to make it clear to himself.

Are you falling in love with this world, or something? He would breathe the cold, strangely scented air, and listen to the slow fall of his horse's hooves on the hard-frozen road, and think. *What's wrong? You've never been here before, why does it all seem so familiar?* But familiar was the wrong word, it was as if, in another life, he had ridden through the hills like these, breathed the cold air and smelled the incense that his companions burned in their campfires in the chilly fog of evening before they slept. For it was new to his eyes, and yet – *it's as if I were a blind man, newly seeing, and everything strange and beautiful and yet just the way I knew it would be* . . .

During these brief interludes when the old Barron came to life in his mind, he realized that this sense of *déjà vu*, of living in a dream, must be some new form of the same hallucinated madness that had cost him his job and his reputation. But these interludes were brief. The rest of the time he rode in the strange dream and enjoyed the sense of suspension between his two worlds and the two selves which he knew he was becoming.

Now the journey would break, and he wondered briefly if the spell would break with it. 'What is Armida?'

Colryn said, 'The estate of the lord Valdir Alton, the Comyn lord who sent for you. He will be pleased that you speak our language fluently, and he will explain to you just what he wishes.' He looked down into the valley, shading his eyes with his hand against the dimming sunlight, and pointed. 'Down there.'

The thick trees, heavy gray-blue conifers that cast dark-spice-smelling small cones on the ground, thinned as they rode downward, and here and there in the underbush some small bird called with perpetual plaintiveness. Thin curls of mist were beginning to take shape in the lowlands, and Barron realized that he was glad they would be indoors before the nightly rain began. He was tired of sleeping on the ground under tarpaulins, though he knew that the climate was mild at this season and that they were lucky it was only rain and not snow. He was tired, too, of food cooked over open fires. He would be glad to sleep under a roof again.

He guided his horse with careless expertness down the slope, letting his eyes fall shut, and drifted off into a brief daydream. *I do not know the Alton lords, and I must keep my real purpose secret from them, until I am certain they would help and not hinder. Here, too, I can find some information about roads and the best way to travel – snow will close the passes soon, and before then I must somehow find the best road to Carthon. The way to the world's end . . .*

He jerked himself out of his daydream He wondered what rubbish was he daydreaming. Where was Carthon, for that matter, *what* was Carthon? As far as he knew, it might be the name of one of the moons! *Oh, hell, maybe I've seen it on a survey map somewhere.* He did look at such things now and then when he had nothing better to do. Perhaps his unconscious – they said the unconscious mind never forgets anything – was weaving dreams with these half-forgotten fragments.

If this went on, he'd be ready for Bedlam. *Ready? Hell, I'm going Tom-o-Bedlam one better!* His brain juggled with scraps of a song learned years ago on another world; it was about the world's end.

'I summoned am to journey
Three leagues beyond the wild world's end,
Methinks it is no journey . . . '

No, that's wrong. He frowned, trying to recapture the words; it fixed his mind on something other than the strangeness around him.

Lerrys drew his horse even. 'Did you say something, Barron?'

'Not really. It would be hard to translate unless – do you understand the Terran language?'

'Well enough,' Lerrys said with a grin.

Barron whistled a scrap of the melody, then sang in a somewhat hoarse but melodious voice:

'With a hose of furious fancies
whereof I am commander,
With a burning spur and a horse of air,
Through the wilderness I wander;
By a queen of air and darkness
I summoned am to tourney
Three leagues beyond the wild world's end;
Methinks it is no journey.'

Lerrys nodded. 'It does seem a little like that sometimes,' he said. 'I like that; so would Valdir. But Armida isn't *quite* at the wild world's end – not yet.'

As he spoke, they rounded a bend; a faint smell of wood smoke and damp earth came up to them from the valley, and through the thin mist they saw the great house lying below them.

'Armida,' said Lerrys, 'my foster father's house.'

Barron did not know just why he had expected it to be a castle, set high among impassable mountain crags, with eagles screaming around the heights. On the downslope, the horses neighed and picked up speed, and Lerrys patted his beast's neck.

'They smell their home and their stable-mates. It was a good trip; I could have come alone. This is one of the safest roads; but my foster father was afraid of dangers by the way.'

'What dangers?' Barron asked. *I must know what I may face on the long road to Carthon.*

Lerrys shrugged. 'The usual things in these hills: cat-men, wandering nonhuman bands, occasional bandits – though they usually prefer wilder country than this, and in any case we aren't enough to tempt the more dangerous ones. And if the Ghost Wind should blow – but I'll be frightening you away.' He laughed. 'This part of the world is peaceful.'

'Have you travelled much?'

'Not more than most,' Lerrys said. 'I crossed the Kilghard Hills leading out of the Hellers with my foster brother, when I was fifteen; but it wasn't any pleasure trip, believe me. And once, I went with a caravan into the Dry Towns, crossing the passes at High Kimbi, beyond Carthon – '

Carthon! The word rank like a bell, kicking something awake in Barron and sending a jolt of adrenalin into his system; he physically twitched, missing the next sentence or two. He said, cutting almost rudely through the younger man's reminiscences, 'Where and what is Carthon?'

Lerrys looked at him strangely. 'A city, or it used to be; it lies well to the east of here. It's almost a ghost town now; no one goes there, but caravans go through the passes; there's an old road, and a ford of the river. Why?'

'I – seem to have heard the name somewhere,' said Barron lamely, and lowered his eyes to his saddle, using as his excuse the horse's increasing pace as the road levelled and led toward the low ramparts of Armida.

Why had he expected it to be a castle? Now that he was at the gates, it seemed reasonable that it should be a wide-flung house, sheltered by walls against the fierce winds from the heights. It was built of blue-gray stone with wide spaces of translucence in the stone walls, behind which lights moved in undefined patches of color and brilliance. They rode through a low arch and into a warm, sheltered courtyard; Barron gave up his horse to a small, swart man clad in fur and leather, who took the reins with a murmured formula of welcome. The Terran slid stiffly to the ground.

Shortly afterward he was beside a high blazing fire in a spacious, stone-flagged hall; lights warred with the dark behind the translucent stone walls and the wind safely shut outside. Valdir Alton, a tall, spare, sharp-eyed man, welcomed Barron with a bow and a few brief formal words; then paused a minute, his eyes resting on the Terran with a sudden, sharp frown.

He said, 'How long have you been on Darkover?'

'Five years.' Barron asked, 'Why?'

'No particular reason, except that – perhaps it is that you speak our language well for such a newcomer. But no man is so young he cannot teach, or so old he cannot learn; we shall be glad to know what you can teach us about the making of lenses. Be welcome to my hearth and my home.' He bowed again and withdrew. Several times during that long evening, the warm and plentiful meal, and the long, lazy period by the fire – which came between the end of supper and the time they were shown to their beds – the Terran felt that the Darkovan lord's eyes were resting on him with a curious intentness.

Some Darkovans are mind-readers, I've heard. If he's read my mind, he must have seen some damn funny things in it. I wonder if there are loose hallucinations running around the planet and I've simply caught a few somehow.

Nevertheless, his sense of confusion did not keep him from eating hugely of the warm, good meal served for the travellers, and enjoying the strange green, resinous wine they drank afterward. The fuzziness from the strong wine seemed to make him less confused about the fuzziness which blurred his surprise at all things Darkovan, and after a while it was pleasant to feel simply drunk instead of feeling that he was watching the scene through two sets of eyes. He sat and sipped the wine from the beautifully carved, green crystal of the goblet, listening to Valdir's young foster daughter Cleindori playing a small harp which she held on her lap, and singing in a soft pentatonic scale some endless ballad about a lake of cloud where stars fell on the shore and a woman walked, showered in stars.

It was good to sleep in the high room hung with translucent curtains and filled with shifting lights; Barron, accustomed to sleeping in a dark room, looked for twenty minutes for a switch to shut them off, then gave up, got into bed and lay watching them drowsily. The shifting colors shifted his mind into neutral gear, and produced colored patterns even behind his closed eyelids, until he slept.

He slept heavily, dreaming strange swooping dreams of flight, watching landscapes tipping and shifting below, and hearing a voice calling in his dreams, again and again, 'Find the road to Carthon! Melitta will await you at Carthon! To Carthon . . . Carthon . . . Carthon . . . '

He woke once, half-dazed, the words still ringing in his ears when he thought sleep had gone. Carthon. Why should he want to go there; and who could make him go? Banishing the thought, he lay down and slept again, only to dream again of the voice that called – murmuring, beseeching, commanding – *'Find the road to Carthon . . . '*

After a long time the dream changed. He was toiling down endless stairs, breaking sharp webs with his outstretched hands, blinded except for a greenish, phosphorescent glow from damp walls that pressed all around him. It was icy cold, and his steps came slow, and his heart beat hard, and the same question pounded in his head: *'Carthon. Where is Carthon?'*

With the sunrise and the thousand small amenities and strangenesses of life in a Darkovan home, he tried to drive the dream away. He wondered again, dispassionately, if he was going mad. *In God's name, what spell has this damned planet woven around me?*

In an attempt to break the bondage of these compelling dreams or sorceries, half through the day, he sought out Lerrys and said to him, 'Your foster father, or whatever he is, was supposed to explain my work to me, and I'm anxious to get started. We Terrans don't like idling around when there is work to be done. Will you ask your father if he can see me now?'

Lerrys nodded. Barron had noticed before that he seemed to be more practical and forthright than the average Darkovan and less concerned with formalities. 'There is, of course, no pressure on you to begin your work at once, but if you prefer it, my guardian and I are at

58

your service whenever you wish. Shall I have your equipment brought up?'

'Please.' Something he had said touched Barron with incongruity. 'I thought Valdir was your father.'

'Foster father.' Again Lerrys appeared to be on the point of saying something, but he withheld it. 'Come, I'll take you to his study.'

It was a smallish room, as Darkovans counted space. Barron thought that at home it would have been a good-sized banquet hall. It looked down on the enclosed court, with alternating layers of glass and translucent stone. It was bitterly cold, although neither Valdir nor Lerrys appeared to suffer from it; the two wore only the linen shirts Darkovan men wore beneath their fur tunics. Outside below them, men were coming and going in the courtyard; Valdir stood and watched them for some minutes, while seeming courteously not to notice how Barron hung over the one small brazier to warm his hands; then he turned back, smiling in welcome.

'Last night in the hall I could give you only formal greetings: I am very glad to see you here, Mr Barron. It was Lerrys and I who arranged that someone from the Terran city should come to teach us something of lens grinding.'

Barron grinned a little sourly. 'It's not my regular work, but I know enough about it to show beginners. So you arranged for me to come here? I thought you people didn't think much of Terran science.'

Valdir gave him a sharp look. He said. 'We have nothing against Terran science. It is Terran *technology* we fear – that Darkover will become just another link in a chain of worlds, all as much alike as sands scattered on the shore, or weeds along the path of the Terrans. But these are matters of politics – or, perhaps, of philosophy, and to be discussed over good wine at night, not offhand while we work together. I think you will find us ready to learn.'

For the last several moments, while he spoke, Barron had been conscious of some low-keyed irritation, like a sound just at the edge of consciousness, which he couldn't quite hear. It made his head ache, and made it hard to hear Valdir's words. He looked around to identify, if he could, what was making the – noise? He couldn't quite hear it. He tried to concentrate on what Valdir was saying; he had missed a sentence or two.

' – and so, you can see, in the foothills, the sight of a sharp–eyed man may be enough, but in the high Sierras, where it's absolutely imperative that any trace of fire must be discovered before it gets out of hand, a lens – what do you call it, a telescope? – would be an invaluable help. It could save acres and acres of timber. Fire in the dry season is such a constant hazard – ' He broke off; Barron was moving his head restlessly from side to side, his hand to his forehead. The sound or vibration or whatever it was seemed to fill every crevice of his skull. Valdir said in surprise, 'The telepathic damper disturbs you?'

'Telepathic which? But *something* seems to be making one hell of a racket in here. Sorry, sir – '

'Not at all,' Valdir said. He went to what looked like an ornamental carving and twisted a knob on it; the invisible noise slackened, and Barron's head quieted to normal. Valdir looked surprised.

'I am sorry; not one Terran in five hundred will know such a device exists, and I had simply forgotten to disconnect it. My deepest apologies, Mr Barron; are you well? Can I offer you anything?'

'No, I'm all right,' Barron said, realizing that he was back to normal again, and wondering what the gadget was. He had the usual Terran notion that Darkover, being a planet without a great deal of manufacturing or technology, was a barbarian one, and the idea of some sort of electronic device functioning out here well beyond the Terran Zone seemed as incongruous as a tree growing in the middle of a spaceport.

'Is this your first trip into the mountains?' Valdir asked.

'No, but the first time I had crossed the plains.' Barron caught himself. What was the matter with him? That gadget and its weird noises seemed to have unsettled his brain. 'Yes, I've never been outside the Terran Zone before this.'

'Of course you haven't seen any real mountains yet,' Lerrys said. 'These are just foothills, really, compared to the Hellers or the Hyades or the Lorillard Ranges.'

'There's quite enough mountain for me,' Barron said. 'If these are foothills, I'm not in any hurry to see anything higher.'

As if to refute what he had said, a picture sprang to swift life in his brain: *I had expected Armida to be like this, a great gray peaked castle lying beneath the chasmed tooth of the mountain, beneath the snow-laden crag with its high plume of snow.*

Barron let his breath out as the picture faded, but before he could think of anything to say, the door opened and Gwynn, now wearing what looked like a green and black uniform, came in, accompanied by two men carrying between them Barron's crate of lens materials and grinding tools. They set it down, under his instructions, and removed the heavy straps, buckles and padding which had protected it on the trip. Valdir thanked the men in an unfamiliar dialect, Gwynn lingered to ask a couple of routine questions, and when the men went away, Barron was once more composed and in possession of himself. *Okay, maybe I've had something like a nervous breakdown in the Terran Zone, and it's still showing in intermittent brainstorms. It doesn't necessarily mean I'm going insane, and it certainly needn't inhibit the work I'm going to be doing.* He was glad to have the chance to collect himself by talking about familiar things.

He had to admit that for men without a standard scientific education, Valdir and Lerrys showed a good deal of comprehension and asked intelligent questions about what he had told them. He gave them a very brief history of lenses – from microscope to telescope to refracting lens for myopia, to binocular lens.

'You realize this is all very elementary,' he added apologetically. 'We've had simple lenses from our prehistory; it's a pre-atomic development on most planets. Now we have the various forms of radar, coherent light devices, and the like. But when men on Terra first started experimenting with light, the lens was our first step in that direction.'

'Oh, it's quite understandable,' said Valdir, 'you needn't apologize. On a planet like Terra, where the random incidence of clairvoyance is so low, it's perfectly natural that men would turn to such experiments.' Barron stared; he hadn't been apologizing.

Lerrys caught his eye and gave Barron a brief, humorous wink, then frowned slightly at his guardian, and Valdir caught himself and continued. 'And of course, it's our good fortune that you have developed this technique. You see, Mr Barron, here on Darkover, throughout *our* pre-history, we were a world where the so-called ESP powers were used, in place of gadgets and machinery, to augment and supplement man's five senses. But so many of these old powers have been lost, or forgotten, during what we call the Years of Chaos, just before the Compact, that now we are forced to supplement our unaided senses with various devices. It's necessary, of course, to be very careful which devices we allow into our society; as the history of all too many planets will show, technology is a two-edged weapon, which can be abused more often than it is used. But we have studied the probable impact on our society quite carefully, and decided that with elementary caution the introduction of lenses will do no palpable harm in the foreseeable future.'

'That's good of you,' said Barron ironically. If Valdir was conscious of the sarcasm he let it pass without comment. He said, 'Larry, of course, has a fairly good technical education, and can make things clear to me if I can't understand. Now, about power sources for your machinery and equipment, Mr Barron. I trust you were warned that very little electricity is available, and only in the lowest of voltages?'

'That's all right. I have mostly hand equipment, and a small generator which can be adapted to work by wind power.'

'Wind is something we have plenty of back here in the mountains,' said Lerrys with a friendly grin. 'I was the one who suggested wind power instead of storage batteries.'

Barron began putting the various bits of equipment back into their case. Valdir rose and went to the window, pausing beside the carved ornament which hid the strange electronic gadget. He asked abruptly, 'Mr Barron, where did you learn to speak Darkovan?'

Barron shrugged. 'I've always been fairly quick at languages.' Then he frowned; he had a good working knowledge of the language spoken in the city near the Trade Zone, but he had given what amounted to a long and fairly technical lecture, without once hesitating, or calling on the young man – Larry or Lerrys or whatever Valdir called him – to interpret. He felt strangely confused and troubled. *Had* he been speaking Darkovan all that time? He hadn't stopped to think what language he was speaking. *Damn it, what is wrong with me?*

'Nothing is wrong,' said Lerrys quickly. 'I told you, Valdir. No I don't understand, either. But – I gave him my knife.'

'It was yours to give, fosterling, but I don't disapprove.'

'Look out,' Lerrys said quickly, 'he can hear us.'

Valdir's sharp eyes swept in the direction of Barron, who suddenly realized that the two Darkovans had been speaking in yet another language. Barron's confusion made him angry. He said, with dry asperity, 'I don't know Darkovan courtesy, but among my people it is considered fairly rude to talk over someone's head, *about* them.'

'I'm sorry,' Lerrys said. 'I had no idea you could hear us, Dan.'

'My foster son, of all people, should know about latent telepaths,' Valdir said. 'I am sorry, Mr Barron; we intended no rudeness. Telepaths, among you Terrans, are not common, though they are not unknown, either.'

'You mean I'm reading your minds?'

'In a sense. It's far too complex a subject to explain in a few minutes. For the moment I suggest you think of it as a very good sort of talent to have for the work you're going to be doing, since it will make it easy for you to talk to people, when you know only a little of their language.'

Barron started to say, *But I'm no telepath, I've never shown any talent for that sort of thing, and when the Rhines gave me the standard psi test for the Space Service, I tested out damn near flat negative.* Then he withheld it. He had been learning a lot about himself lately, and it was certain that he wasn't the same man he had been before. If he developed a few talents to go with his hallucinations, that was perhaps the law of compensation in action. It had certainly made it easier to talk to Valdir, so why complain?

He finished carefully putting the equipment in the crate, and listened to Valdir's assurances that it would be securely wrapped and crated for the trip up to the mountain station where he would be working. But when, a few minutes later, he took his leave and went down the hall, he was shocked and yet unsurprised to realize that the voices of Valdir and Lerrys continued, like distant whispers inside his head.

'*Do you suppose the Terrans chose a telepath purposely?*'

'*I don't think so, Foster Father; I don't believe they knew enough about choosing or training them. And he seems too surprised by the whole thing. I told you that from somewhere he had picked up an image of Sharra.*'

'*Sharra, of all conceivable!*' – Valdir's mental voice blurted out in astonishment and what seemed like dismay. '*So you gave him your knife, Larry! Well, you know what that will mean. I'll release you from your pledge, if you like; tell him who you are when it seems necessary.*'

'*It's not because he's a Terran. But if he's going to be running around Darkover in that state, someone's got to do something about it – and I can probably understand him better than most people. It isn't all that easy, to change worlds.*'

'*Don't jump to conclusions, Larry. You don't know that he's changing worlds.*'

Larry's tone in answer sounded positive, and yet somehow sad. '*Oh, yes, he will. Where would he go among the Terrans, after this?*'

—— 6 ——

Melitta crept down the long, tunneled stairway, groping through the darkness. After the faint light from the cracks behind her had died, she was in total darkness and had to feel each step with her feet before setting her weight on it. She wished she had thought to bring a light. But on the other hand, she would need both hands to find her way and to brace herself. She went carefully, never putting her full weight on a step without testing it. She had never been down here before, but her childhood had been soaked in stories of her Storn forefathers and the builders of the castle before them, and she knew that secret exits and tunnels could be honeycombed with nasty surprises for people who blundered through them without appropriate precautions.

Her care was not superfluous. Before she had gone more than a few thousand feet down into the darkness, the wall at her left hand fell away and left her feeling a breath of dank air which seemed to rise out of an immense depth. The air was moving, and she had no fear of suffocation, but the echoes stirred at such distance that she quailed at the thought of that drop to her left; and when she dislodged a small pebble with her foot and it slipped over the edge it seemed to fall forever before landing at last, a distant whisper, far below.

Abruptly her hands struck cold stone and she found that she had run into a blank wall. Taken aback for a moment, she began to feel about and discovered that she was inching, foot by foot, along a narrow shelf at the foot of the stairs. She felt her hands strike and break thick webs, and cringed at the thought of the unseen creatures in the darkness that had spun them; she had no fear of ordinary spiders, but who could tell what horrors might spawn here, out of sunlight since the beginning of the world, and what they would crawl over in the darkness and what ghastly things they would find to eat. She braced herself, setting her small chin, thinking. *They won't get to eat me, anyhow*. She gripped the hilt of her knife and held it before her.

To her left, a small chink of pale greenish light wavered. Could she have come to the end of the tunnel already? It was no normal daylight or moonlight. Wherever the light came from, it was not outside. The ledge suddenly widened and she could step back and walk at ease instead of inching along.

The greenish light grew slowly, and now she saw that it came through an arched doorway at the end of the stone passageway along which she walked. Melitta was far from timid, but there was something about that green light which she disliked before she saw more than a glimmer of it, something which seemed to go beneath the roots of consciousness and stir old half-memories which lay at the very depths of her being. Darkover was an old world and the mountains were the most ancient bones of the world, and no man knew what might have crawled beneath the mountains when the sun first began to cool, ages ago, there to lie and grow in unseen horror.

She had been walking silently in her fur-lined boots; now she ghosted along hardly disturbing the air she walked through, holding her breath for fear it would disturb some hidden *something*. The green light grew stronger, and, although it was still no brighter than moonlight, somehow it hurt her eyes so that she slitted them to narrowness against it and tried not to let it inside her eyelids. There was something very awful down here.

Well, she thought, *even if it's a dragon, it can't be much worse than Brynat's men. At worst a dragon would only want to eat me. Anyhow, there haven't been any dragons on Darkover for a thousand years. They were all killed off before the Ages of Chaos.*

The doorway from which the green light emanated was very near. She felt the poisonous brightness as a positive assault on her eyes. She stepped to the doorway and peered through, holding her breath against screaming at the ghastly glare which lay ahead.

She could see that the green light came from some thick, poisonous fungus that grew in the slow currents of air. The room ahead was high and arched, and she could see carvings covered with fungus, and at the far end, blurred and overgrown shapes which had once been a dais and something like chairs.

Melitta took a firm hold of her nerves. *Why should it be evil just because it's green and slimy-looking,* she demanded of herself. *So is a frog, and frogs are harmless. So was the moss on a rock. Why should plants growing in their own way give me this overwhelming feeling of something wicked and sinister?* Nevertheless, she could not make her feet move to take the first step into that arched room. The green light made her eyes ache, and there was a faint smell, as if of carrion.

Slowly, as her eyes grew accustomed to the green, she saw the things that crawled among the fungus.

They were white and sluggish. Their eyes, great and curiously iridescent, moved slowly in her direction, and the girl felt her stomach heave at that blind regard. She stood there paralyzed, thinking frantically, *This must be new, they can't have been here all along, this passage was in good shape forty years ago; I remember my father speaking of it, though he hadn't been down here since years before I was born.*

She stood back, studying the green stalactites of fungus and the crawling things. They looked dreadful, but were they dangerous as well? Even though they made her skin crawl, they might be as harmless as most spiders. Perhaps, if she could simply summon up the nerve to run through them, that was all that was needed.

A small restless rustle behind her made her look down. Near her skirts, sitting up on his hind legs and surveying her with curiosity, a small red-furred rodentlike animal hung back from entering the cave. He gave a small, nervous chitter which seemed to Melitta to mirror her own apprehension. He was a dirty-looking little creature, but by contrast with the things in the green cave he looked normal and friendly. Melitta almost smiled at him.

He squeaked again and, with a sudden burst of speed, set off running through the fungus.

The green branches whipped down on the little creature. It screamed thinly and was still, smothered in the green, which seemed to pulse with ghastly light. Through the phosphorescence the small golden-eyed horrors moved, swarmed, and moved away. Not even the bones were left; there was only an infinitesimal scrap of pinkish fur.

Melitta crammed her fist in her mouth to keep from screaming. She took a convulsive step backward, watching the slow subsiding of the fungus. It took some minutes to subside.

After a long time her heartbeat slowed to normal and she found herself frantically searching for solutions. *I wish I could get through here somehow and lure Brynat's men down after me,* she thought grimly, but that line seemed to go nowhere.

Fire. All living things fear fire, except man. If I could carry fire . . .

She had no light; but she did have steel and tinder in her pocket; on Darkover to be outdoors without the means of making fire in the snow season, was to die. Before she was eight years old she had known all the tricks of firemaking anywhere and everywhere.

Trying not to breathe hard, she pulled out her fire-making materials. She had nothing she could use for a torch, but she tore off her scarf, wound it round a small slab of rock; and set it alight. Then, carrying it carefully in front of her, she stepped into the fungus cave.

The green branches whipped back as the firelight and heat struck them. The sluggish crawling at her feet made her gasp with horror, but they made no effort to attack, and she began to breathe again as she began to walk, steadily, across the cave. She must go quickly but not too fast to see where she was going. The scarf would not burn more than a minute at most. Fortunately the patch of green seemed to be less than a hundred yards; beyond the further arch was darkness again.

One of the crawling things struck her foot. It felt squishy, like a frog, and she gasped, staggered a little for balance, and dropped the blazing scarf. She swooped to retrieve it . . .

A high shrill yeeping came from the crawling thing. The green fungus near her feet moved, and Melitta held her breath and waited for it to strike.

The blazing scarf touched the green branch and it caught fire. A blaze of ghastly green-red light licked up to the ceiling; Melitta felt the blast of heat as the fire blazed up, catching branch after branch. In half a minute the walls of the cave were ablaze; the small crawling things screamed, writhed and died at her feet as the green branches, agitating violently, struggled to get out of range, were caught by the blaze and burned.

It seemed an eternity that she stood there in terror, trying to draw her clothing back from the flames, her ears hurting with the screams and her eyes burning from the greenish tint of the fire. Rationally she knew that it must have been only a few minutes before the flames, finding nothing more to feed on, sank and died, leaving her alone in unrelieved, blessed darkness.

She began to move slowly across the cave, in the remembered direction of the other door, holding her breath and trying not breathe the scorched, poisonous dust of the burnt fungus. Under her feet it crumpled unpleasantly and she hated setting her feet on the ground, but there was no help for it. She kept moving, numbly, in the direction of that remembered patch of darkness beyond the fungus cave.

She knew when she had passed through it, for almost at once the air was cleaner, and under her feet there was nothing but hard rock. There was also faint light from somewhere – a glimmer of moonlight, perhaps, from a hidden airshaft. The air felt cool and sweet; the builders of these tunnels had gone to some pains to make them pleasant to walk in. Far off she heard a trickle of water, and, her throat still full of the dust of the burnt fungus, it was like a promise.

She went down, moving toward the sound of distant water, Twice she shrank, seeing on the walls a trace, hardly more than a smear, of the greenish stuff, and made a mental note, *If I ever get back I'll come down and burn it out. If not, I hope it grows fast – and Brynat comes down here some day!*

After what seemed like hours of slow descent she found the water – a trickling stream coming out of the rock and dripping slowly down along the stairs beside her path. She cupped her hands and drank. The water was good, and she drank well, cleansed her grimy face, and ate a few bites of food. She could tell, by the feel of the air on her face, that the night was far advanced. She must be safely hidden by morning.

Must I? I could lie hidden in the tunnel for a day or two, till pursuit quiets.

Then she knew she could not. She simply could not trust Allira that much. Her sister would not intentionally betray her; but if Brynat suspected Allira knew, he would try anything to extract the information from her. She had no faith in Allira's ability to resist questioning for any length of time.

As she went downward, she realized that the slope of the tunnel was lessening, until she walked on a grade that was just downhill. She must be coming near the end of the long stair. She was a fair judge of distances, and she knew that she had walked a considerable distance in the night; the tunnel must have led far beneath the castle and down into the caves and cliffs beneath. Then she came upon a great pair of bronze doors, thrust them outward, and stood in the open air, free.

It was still dark although the smell of the air told her that dawn was less than two hours away. The moons had set, and the rain had stopped, though mist still lay along the ground. She looked back at the closed doors behind her.

She knew where she was now. She had seen these doors from the outside when as a child she played in the forge village. She stood now in an open square of stone, surrounded on every side by the doors cut in the cliffs that rose around her. The sky was only a narrow cut above. She looked at the dark house doors, some of them still agape, and thought with all the longing in her weary body of how good it would be to crawl into one of the abandoned houses to lie down and sleep for hours.

She forced herself upright again and went down the path that led between the cliffs. Like the tunnel, the empty forge village would be the first place searched if Brynat managed to force the secret of the passage from Allira. She passed the open-air hearths where countless years ago, smiths had worked, making their beautiful and curious ironwork, copper jewelry and the iron gates of their own castle now crumpled and thrown down in the siege. She cast a look upward. From here she could see a portion of the outworks. Brynat had spared no time in repairing the fortifications of Storn. Evidently he thought he might have to hold them against invaders.

He will, I swear it by Avarra and Zandru, I swear it by Sharra, Goddess of Forges and Fires! He shall struggle tenfold . . .

There was no time for that. If she wanted to make Brynat suffer, there was only one way to achieve it, she must get away herself. Her own safety must be the first thought. She passed the old circle of fireplaces, cold and rusted. Even the carven image of Sharra above the central forge was dulled and the gold of her chains, set against the duller metal of the statue, covered with spiderwebs and bird-droppings. She flinched at the sacrilege. She was no worshipper of the Flamehair, but like every child of the mountains, she had a deep respect and awe for the secret arts of the smith.

If I come back — when I come back Sharra's image shall be purified and served again . . . There was no time for that now, either.

The horizon was reddening perceptibly when footsore Melitta, her steps dragging, clung to the doorway of a small house in a village far below the castle, and beat weakly on it. She felt at her last strength. If no one heard

71

her or helped her, she would fall down here and lie there until Brynat's men found her, or she died.

But it was not more than a few moments until the door opened a cautious crack, and then motherly arms grasped her and drew her inside and to a fire.

'Quick – bar the door, draw the curtain – *damisela*, where did you come from? We thought you dead in the siege, or worse! How did you get free? Evanda guard us! Your poor hands, your face – Reuel, you oaf, bring some wine, quickly, for our little lady.'

A few minutes later, drinking hot soup, her boots drawn off and her feet to the fire, wrapped in blankets, Melitta was telling a little of her escape to a wide-eyed audience.

'Lady, you must hide here until the search is quiet – ' but their faces were apprehensive, and Melitta said a swift 'No. Brynat would surely kill you all,' and saw shamed relief in their eyes. 'I can lie hidden in the caves up the mountain until darkness tonight; then I can get away to Nevarsin or beyond. But you can find me food to carry, and perhaps a horse that can face the passes.'

It was quickly arranged and by the time the day broke, Melitta rested, wrapped in furs and rugs in the labyrinthine caves which had for centuries been a last hiding place of the Storns. For one day she was safe there, since Brynat would surely search nearer places first; and by tonight she would be gone. It was a long road to Carthon.

Exhausted, the girl slept, but the name tolled in her dreams – *Carthon*.

Barron had believed, on the journey from the Terran Zone to Armida, that he had seen mountains. True, his Darkovan escort had repeatedly called them foothills, but he had put that down to exaggeration, to the desire to see the stranger's surprise. Now, half a day's ride from Armida, he began to see that they had not exaggerated. As they came out of a miles–long, sloping pathway along a forested hill, he saw, lying before him, the real ranges: Cool purple, deep violet, pale grayed blue, they lay there fold on fold and height behind height, each successive fold rising higher and farther away, until they vanished in cloudy distances that might have been thunderheads – or further ranges.

'Good God,' he exploded, 'we're not going over the top of *those*, are we?'

'Not quite,' Colryn, riding at his side, reassured him. 'Only to the peak of the second range, there.' He pointed. 'The fire tower is on the crest of that range.' He told Barron its name in Darkovan. 'But if you look far enough, you can see all the way back into the mountains, as far as the range they call the Wall Around the World. Nobody lives beyond there, except the trailmen.'

Barron remembered vague stories of various groups of Darkovan nonhumans. The next time they paused to eat cold food from their saddlebags and rest the horses, he looked for Lerrys, who was still the friendliest of the three, and asked him about them. 'Are they only beyond the far ranges? Or are there nonhumans in these mountains too?'

'Oh, yes. You've been on Darkover how long, five of

our years, and you still haven't seen any of our non-humans?'

'One of two *kyrii* in the Terran Trade Zone – from a distance,' Barron told him, 'and the little furred people at Armida – I don't know what you call them. Are there others? And are they all – well, if they're nonhumans, I can't ask, "are they human," but do they meet Empire standards for so-called intelligent beings – time-binding culture, viable language capable of transfer to other I.B.'s?'

'Oh, they're all I.B.'s by Terran Empire standards,' Lerrys assured him. 'The reasons the Empire doesn't deal with them is fairly simple. Humans here don't have much interest in the Empire *per se*, but they are interested in other humans as individuals. The nonhuman races – I'm no expert on them, but I suspect they have never tried to get in touch with the Empire for the same reason they don't have much contact with humans on Darkover. Their goals and wishes and so forth are so completely different that there's no point of contact; they don't want any and they don't have any.'

'You mean even Darkovans have no contact with non-humans?'

'I wouldn't say *no* contact. There's some small amount of trade with the trailmen – they're what you might call half-human or subhuman, and they live in the trees in the forests. They trade with the mountain people for drugs, small tools, metal and the like. They're harmless enough unless you frighten them. The catmen – they're a race something like the *cralmacs*, the furred servants at Armida. *Cralmacs* aren't very intelligent; feline rather than simian, but they do have culture of a sort, and some of them are telepathic. Their level is about that of a moron, or a chimpanzee who suddenly acquired a tribal culture. A genius among the *cralmacs* might learn a dozen words of a human language but I never heard of one learning to read; I suspect the Empire people gave them pretty wide benefit of the doubt in classifying them as I.B.'s'

'We tend to do that. We don't want later squawks that

we treated a potential intelligent race as higher animals.'

'I know. *Cralmacs* are listed as real or potential I.B.'s and let alone. The catmen, I suspect, are a hell of a lot more intelligent; I know they use metal tools. Fortunately I've never been close to them; they hate men and they'll attack when they feel safe in doing it. I've heard that they have a very elaborate feudal culture with the most incredible tangle of codes governing face-saving behavior. The Dry-towners believe that some of the elements of their own culture came from cultural interchange with the catmen millennia ago, but an I.B. xenthropologist could tell you more about that.'

'Just how many races of I.B.'s are there on Darkover anyway?' Barron asked.

'God only knows, and I'm not being funny. Certainly no Terran knows. Maybe a few of the Comyn know, but they're not telling. Or the *chieri*; they're another of the nearly human races, but they're as far above humans, most people think, as the *cralmacs* are below 'em. It's for sure no Terran knows, though; and I've had more opportunity than most.'

Barron hardly heard the last sentence for a minute, in his interest in the nonhumans, then suddenly it penetrated. '*You're* a Terran?'

'At your service. My name is Larry Montray; they call me Lerrys because it's easier for a Darkovan to pronounce, that's all.'

Barron felt suddenly angry and irked. 'And you let me make a fool of myself trying to speak Darkovan to you?'

'I offered to interpret,' Larry said. 'At the time I was under a pledge to Valdir, never to mention that I was a Terran – not to anyone.'

'And you're his ward? His foster son? How'd that happen?'

'It's a long story,' Larry said. 'Some other time, maybe.* In brief, his son, Kennard, is being schooled on Terra with *my* family, and I'm living here with *his* people.'

*cf. *Star of Danger*.

He scrambled to his feet. 'Look, Gwynn's looking for us; I think we ought to get on. We want to reach the fire tower before nightfall tomorrow, if we can – the rangers there are due to be relieved – and it's still a long way into those hills.'

It gave Barron plenty to think about, as they rode on, but his thoughts kept coming back, with an insistence he could not understand – it was as if some secret watcher, far back in his mind, kept dwelling on that point almost with frenzy.

A Terran could pass as a Darkovan. A Terran could pass as a Darkovan. A Darkovan could pass himself off as a Terran. A Terran could pass as a Darkovan. In these mountains, where Terrans are never seen, a Terran willing to pass as a Darkovan would be safe from anything human, and attract no unusual attention from nonhumans . . .

Barron shook his head. *That's enough of that.* He wasn't interested in the Darkovan mountains except from the viewpoint of doing his job well enough to redeem himself with the Empire, and get his own job, or something like it, back, and start over again on another planet, in a spaceport job. If Larry, or Lerrys, or whatever he calls himself, wants to amuse himself living with a family of weird, Darkovan telepaths and learning more than anyone else cared to know about nonhuman and such, that's his business; everybody gets their kicks in his own way and I've known some dillies. But he wasn't having any.

He clung to that with an uneasy concentration all that day, doggedly ignoring the beauty of the flowers that lined the mountain road, snubbing Larry's friendly attempts to pick up the conversation. Toward evening, as the ride steepened. Colryn whiled away the time by singing Darkovan legends in a tuneful bass voice, but Barron shut his ears and would not listen, closing his eyes and letting his horse take the road along the mountain trail; the horse knew more about it than he did.

The sound of hoofs, the slow jogging in the saddle, the darkness behind his closed eyes, was first hypnotic, then strangely familiar; it seemed normal to sit unseeing in his saddle, trusting himself to the horse beneath him and his other senses alert – the smell of flowers, or conifers, of the dust of the road, the sharp scent of some civet-smelling animal in the brush. When Lerrys drew abreast of him, Barron kept his eyes closed and after a time Lerrys spurred his horse and overtook Colryn. Colryn went on singing in an undertone. Without knowing how he knew, Barron recognized that the singer had shifted to the opening bars of the long *Ballad of Cassilda*.

How strange it sounded without the water-harp accompaniment. Allira played and sang it well though it was really a song for a man's voice:

> The stars were mirrored on the shore,
> Dark was the dark enchanted moor,
> Silent as cloud or wave or stone,
> Robardin's daughter walked alone.
> A web of gold between her hands
> On shining spindle burning bright,
> Deserted lay the mortal lands
> When Hastur left the realms of light.
> Then, singing like a hidden bird . . .

He lost track of the words, hearing a far-off hawk-cry and the small wounded scream of some animal in the bush. *He was here, he was free, and behind him, ruin and death.*
The song went on, soft and incessant;

> . . . A hand to each, he faltering came
> Within the hidden mountain hall
> Where Alar tends the darkened flame
> That brightened at Cassilda's call . . .
> And as his brilliance paled away
> Into the dimmer mortal day.
> Cassilda left the shining loom,
> A starflower in his hand she laid;
> Then on him fell a mortal doom:
> He rose and kissed Robardin's maid.

The golden webs unwoven lay . . .

His mind spun in a strange dream as he listened to the song of the love of Cassilda, the sorrows of Camilla, the love of Hastur and the treachery of Alar. *It must be strange to be Comyn and Hastur, and know oneself sib to the God . . .*

I could use a god or two for kinsmen now!

What are these old gods really? The forge people used to say that Sharra came to their fires — and they didn't mean the spirit of fire, either! The old telepaths could raise powers as far beyond my bird forms, or the fire shields, as these are beyond a trailman's knife!

'Barron! Don't fall asleep here, man; the trail gets dangerous!' The voice of Gwynn, the big Darkovan, broke into his dream, and Barron shook himself awake. Was it another hallucination? – No, only a dream. 'I must have been asleep,' he said, rubbing his eyes. Gwynn chuckled. 'And to think that five days ago you'd never been in the saddle. You learn fast, stranger. Congratulations! But you'd better keep your eyes open from here; the path gets rough and narrow, and you probably have better judgment than your horse – even though there *is* an old proverb that says, "on an uphill road give your horse his head." But if you fell here – ' He gestured at the thousand-foot drop on either side of the pass. 'We ought to try and get through and down into the valleys, before nightfall. There are Ya-men around these heights, and perhaps banshees; and although there's no sign of the Ghost Wind, I'm not any too eager to meet them just the same.'

Barron started to ask what they were and stopped himself. *Damn it, I don't care; I'm already too entangled in this business, and Gwynn and the others are here to guard me.* There was no reason he should think about these supposed dangers or even know what they were.

Nevertheless, the unease of the others penetrated to him, and he found himself pulling close to them in the narrow neck of the pass. It was almost an anti-climax when they topped the pass without incident and began to ride downward.

78

They camped that night in the valley under a shelter of the gray–blue boughs, which smelled of spice and rain; there was less talk and singing than usual. Barron, lying awake in his blankets and listening to the nightly rain sliding off the thick boughs, felt an apprehension he could not check. *What a hell of a world, and why did I have to get stuck in it?*

Already he had half forgotten the delight and fascination he had felt during the first journey through the foothills. It was part of that strangeness within which he wanted to forget.

They arrived at the ranger station late the next day; Barron, unpacking his crates by lamplight in the large, airy room allotted to him, realized grudgingly that at least Valdir had spared no pains to make a guest comfortable. There were ample shelves and cupboards for his working tools, benches and space with good light – the pressure lamps produced unusual amounts of light from the relatively crude fuels extracted from resins and oils of the local trees. A broad window of clear glass – not common on Darkover, not much desired, and evidently provided for the comfort of the Terran guest – provided an unbelievable panoramic view of mountains, and ridge after ridge of forested and rocky slopes and heights. As Barron stood at the window, watching the huge red sun of Darkover setting behind the peak – the mountains here were so high that the sun was hidden even before the night's mist formed – he was touched again with that uncanny sense which made his heart race; but by sheer force of will he kept himself from succumbing to it, and went out to explore the station.

From where it sat at the top of one of the tallest peaks, it commanded a view – even without climbing to the tower behind – of what seemed like hundreds of square miles of forested country; Barron counted fifteen small villages, each lying sheltered in a fold of the hills, each only a cluster of dim roofs. At this distance he could see why telescopes would be needed; the view stretched so far that it vanished in haze through which no unaided eye could penetrate and which could easily hide a thin coil of smoke. He could even see the faraway roofs of Armida, and, high in the hills, a dim pale spire which looked like a castle.

'With your lenses,' Larry told him, joining him at the doorway of the station, 'we will see forest fires while they are still only small blazes, and save our timber. Look.' He pointed to the side of a faraway ridge which was a black scar in the green. 'That burned five years ago; it was out of control only for a day or two, but even though every man from seven villages turned out, we lost I forget how many square miles of good timber and resin trees. Also, from here, we could see and give the warning, if bandits or something attacked.'

'How do you give warning? There seem to be no sirens or any such things here.'

'Bells, fire beacons – ' He pointed to a high pile of dry weed carefully isolated behind a ditch filled with water, 'And also, signaling devices – I don't think I ever knew the Terran name for them.' He showed Barron the shiny metal plates. 'Of course they can only be used on sunny days.'

'Heliograph,' Barron said.

'That's it.'

Barron had expected to feel like a fish out of water, but the first few days went smoothly enough. There were six men at the ranger station, serving tours of duty of fifteen days each and then being replaced by others, in a staggered rotation system which sent three new men every seven days. Currently Gwynn was in command of the station. Larry seemed a sort of supernumerary, and Barron wondered if he was there only to interpret, or to keep an eye on the stranger. From something Gwynn said, he eventually decided that Larry was there to learn the management of the station, so that he could take his place in a series of responsible duties held in sequence by all younger men of Darkovan families. Colryn was there as Barron's assistant, specifically to learn the work of lens-grinding and to teach the making and use of the telescopes and lenses to any of the rangers who were willing to learn.

Barron knew, from his orientation lectures years ago, that Darkover was a world without complex technology or industry, and he had expected that the Darkovans would not be very adept at learning what he had come to teach. He was surprised to see the swiftness with which Colryn and the others picked up the rudiments of optics, his instructions on the properties of reflected and refracted light, and later, the technical work of grinding. Colryn in particular was apt at picking up the technical language, the meticulous scientific techniques; so was Larry, who hung around when he was not out on patrol, but then Barron had expected it of Larry, who was a Terran and seemed to have at least the rudiments of a Terran education. But Colryn was a surprise.

He said as much one afternoon, when they were working in the upstairs workroom; he had been showing the younger man how to set and adjust one of the complex grinding tools and how to check it with the measuring instruments for proper set. 'You know, you really don't need me,' he said. 'You could have picked this up on your own with a couple of textbooks. It was hardly worth Valdir's trouble to bring me all the way out here; he could simply have gotten books and equipment from the Terran Zone and turned them over to you.'

Colrun shrugged; 'He'd have to have me taught to read 'em first.'

'You can speak some Terran Standard; you wouldn't have that much trouble learning. As nearly as I can tell, the Darkovan script isn't so complicated that you'd have any difficulty with Empire letters.'

Colryn laughed this time. 'I couldn't say. Maybe if I could read at all, I could read Terran Standard. It's nothing I've ever stopped to think about.'

Barron stared in frank shock; Colryn *seemed* intelligent enough! He looked at Larry, expecting to exchange a look of consternation at this barbarous planet; but Larry frowned slightly and said, almost in reproof, 'We don't make a fetish of literacy on Darkover, Barron.'

Suddenly he felt condemnatory and like a stranger

again. He almost snarled. 'How in the hell does anyone learn anything, then?'

He could see Colryn visibly summoning up patience and courtesy toward the boorish stranger, and felt ashamed. Colryn said, 'Well, I'm learning, am I not? Even though I'm no sandal-wearer, to sit and wear my eyes out over printed pages!'

'You're certainly learning. But you mean you have no system of education?'

'Probably not the way you mean it,' said Colryn. 'We don't bother with writing unless we're in the class that has to spend their time reading and writing. We've found that too much reading spoils the eyes – weren't you telling me, a few days ago, that about eighty per cent of your Terrans have imperfect vision and have to wear false lenses to their eyes? It would seem to make more sense to set those people to doing work which doesn't need so much reading – anyway, too much writing things down spoils the memory; you don't remember a thing properly if you can go and look it up. And when I want to learn something, why should I not learn it the sensible way, from someone who can show me if I am doing it properly, without the intermediary of printed symbols between us? With only a book to learn from, I might misunderstand and get in the way of doing things wrong, whereas here, if I make a mistake you can set me right at once, and the skill gets into my hands, so that my hands will remember how the work is done.'

Not really convinced, Barron let the discussion drop. He had to admit that the arguments were singularly coherent for someone he now had to reclassify as an illiterate. His systems of thinking were shaken up; communications devices had always been his field. Colryn said, evidently trying to bend over backward and see his point of view, 'Oh, I didn't say there was anything *wrong* with reading, in itself. If I were deaf or crippled, I'm sure I would find it useful – ' But understandably, this did not calm Barron's ruffled feelings.

Not for worlds would he have admitted what was really

bothering him most at the moment. His hands went on, with almost automatic skill, adjusting the delicate micrometric measurements on the grinding tool, and connecting it to the small wind-powered generator. While Colryn was talking, the argument somehow seemed *familiar*. It was as if he had heard it all before, in some other life! He thought, with black humor, that if this went on, he would come to believe in reincarnation!

His eyes blurred before him, colors running into one another and blearing into unfamiliar patches, shapes and groups without reference. He looked at the equipment in his hands as if he had never seen it before. He turned the pronged plug curiously in his hands; what was he supposed to do with this thing? As it focused and came clear, he found that he was staring wildly at Colryn, and Colryn looked strange to him.

All the strange colors flooded together again and sight went out; he found himself standing on a great height, looking down at a scene of ruin and carnage, hearing men shrieking, and swords clashing. As it blotted out sight, he found himself once again looking up at rushing flames, and in the midst of the fire was a smiling woman, flame-haired, lapped in fire as another woman might stand beneath a waterfall. Then the woman faded and was only a great female shape, fire-crowned and golden-chained . . .

'Barron!' The cry cut through his consciousness and he came briefly back, rubbing his eyes, to see Colryn and Larry staring at him in consternation. Larry caught the lens machines from his hands as he swayed and crashed to the floor.

When he came to himself again, water trickling down his throat, they were both staring down at him with troubled concern in their faces. Colryn was apologetic. 'I think you've been working too hard. I shouldn't have gotten into that argument with you: you have your ways and we have ours. Have you had seizures like this often?'

Barron simply shook his head. The argument hadn't bothered him that much, and if Colryn wanted to explain it away as an epileptic fit or something of that sort, that was all right with him and probably a saner explanation than whatever it really was. Perhaps he was suffering some sort of brain damage! *Oh, well, at least when it happens out here in the Darkovan mountains, I'm not likely to be responsible for crashing a couple of spaceships!*

Colryn might have accepted this explanation but it was quickly obvious that Larry hadn't. He sent Colryn away, saying that he was sure Barron wouldn't feel like working for the rest of the day; then he began slowly to put the lens-grinding equipment away. Barron started to get up and help him, and Larry gestured to him to stay put.

'I can manage; I know where this stuff goes. Barron, what do you know of Sharra?'

'Nothing – less than nothing.' *It's damned unhandy having a telepath around.* 'You tell me.'

'I don't know that much. She was an ancient goddess of the forge people. But gods and goddesses, here on Darkover, are more than just something you say your prayers to, or burn incense to, or ask for favors. They seem to be real – tangible, I mean.'

'That sounds like rubbish, gobbledygook.'

'I mean, what they call gods, we'd call forces – real, solid forces you can touch. For instance – I don't know much about Sharra. The Darkovans, especially in the Comyn, don't like to talk about Sharra worship. It was outlawed years ago; it was thought to be too dangerous. Also, it seemed to involve human sacrifice, or something like it. What I mean is, the forge people called on Sharra, using the proper talisman or whatever – these things concentrate forces, I don't know how – and Sharra would bring the metallic ore up out of the mountains for them.'

'And you a Terran? And you believe all that suff? Larry, there are legends like that on every planet in the Empire.'

'Legend be damned,' said Larry. 'I told you I don't think they're gods as we use the term. They may be some form of – well, entity or being – maybe from some other dimension. For all I know, they could be an invisible race of nonhumans. Valdir told me a little about the outlawing of Sharra worship – it happened here in the mountains. His people, the Altons and the Hasturs, had a lot to do with it; they had to go into the hills and confiscate all the talismans of Sharra so that the forge people couldn't call up these forces any more. Among other things, I gather, the fires sometimes got out of control and started forest fires.'

'Talismans?'

'Stones — they call them matrix stones — blue crystals, I've learned to use them a little; believe me, they're weird. If you have even rudimentary telepathic force, you concentrate your thoughts on them and they — well, they do things. They can lift objects — psychokinesis — create magnetic fields, create force-field locks that no one can open except with the same matrix, and so forth. My foster sister could tell you more about them.' Larry looked distressed. 'Valdir should know, if Sharra images can even get to you, a Terran. I should send to him, Barron.'

Barron shook his head urgently. 'No! Don't trouble Valdir; this is my problem.'

'No trouble. Valdir will want to know. Valdir is of the Comyn. He *must* know if these things are coming into the mountains again. They could be dangerous for us all, and especially for you.' He smiled a troubled smile. 'I shared a knife with you, and it is a pledge,' he said. 'I have to stand your friend whether you want me to or not. I'll send for Valdir tonight.'

He finished closing the box with the lens blanks, and turned to go. 'You'd better rest; nothing is urgent, and I have to go out on patrol,' he said. 'And don't worry; it is probably nothing to do with you. You have evidently picked up something that is loose in these mountains, and Valdir will know how to deal with it.' He paused at the door, said urgently, 'Please believe that we are your friends, Barron.' He left.

Alone, Barron lay on the wide bed, that smelled of the resin–needles used to stuff the mattress. He wondered why it seemed so urgent to him that Valdir should not be sent for. He heard Larry ride away with the patrol; he heard Colryn singing downstairs; and he heard the wind rise and begin blowing from the heights. He got up and went to the wide window. Down in these valleys and hills lay villages of unsuspecting men, little knots and nests of nonhumans in the thickest and most impenetrable forests, and birds and wildlife; they would be safer for protection against forest fire and raiding bandits – catmen and nonhumans and the terrible Ya-men. He would help with that, he was doing good work; why then was he gripped by this sense of fearful urgency and despair, as if he sat idling while around him a world fell into ruins? Disoriented, he covered his eyes.

It was quiet at the station. He knew that in the tower a ranger in the usual green and black uniform scanned the surrounding countryside for any signs of smoke; the resin trees, in spite of the nightly rain, were so volatile, that an unexpected thunderstorm could strike one and send it ablaze. The only sound was the wind that never changed and never died; Barron hardly heard it now. And yet there was something – something in the wind . . .

He tensed, throwing the window open and leaning out, closing his eyes the better to focus attention.

It was almost imperceptible except to senses sharpened like his – almost lost in the overpowering smell of the resins – a faint, sweet, yellow-dusty smell, almost lost, borne on the wind . . .

The Ghost Wind! Pollen of a plant which flowered erratically only once in several seasons – was released in enormous quantities, scattering its scent and queer hallucinogenic qualities from the valleys to the heights; blessedly rare, it produced euphoria and a queer drunkenness and, occasionally, if one breathed too much of it, brain damage in men. It released the animal instincts of rage and fear and anger, sending men cowering in corners or raving on the hills. But into the nonhumans it went deeper, penetrating into their strange brains and releasing very old things, very terrible things . . . The catmen would howl and strike and kill wantonly, and the Ya-men – when it reached the Ya-men –

He moved fast. He was not Barron now; he was not conscious of himself or who or what he was, he knew only that he must act to warn the others at the station, to warn the men in the valleys to take shelter. It would not be strong enough for any ordinary nose to smell for two or three more hours, and by that time the rangers would be too far from the station to take shelter, and the nonhumans would already be out and ravening. By the time the Ghost Wind was strong enough to affect humans it might even be too late to take shelter.

His vision was blurring. He closed his eyes, the better to let his feet find their way around, and ran down the stairs. He heard someone call to him in an unfamiliar language, pushed past and ran on.

The beacon. He might light the beacon! He did not know the alarm systems here but the beacon would certainly alert everyone in danger. There was a fire burning in the lower hall, he could feel its heat on his face. He bent over, carefully reaching, picked out a long stick blazing at one end and cool and charred at the other. He ran with it in his hand out the door and across the graveled horse path and the lawn; almost falling into the ditch around the beacon, he thrust the blazing torch into the tinder-dry wood and leaped back as it flamed up and a tall column of fire reared to the sky. Then someone yelled at him, hands were gripping him, and Colryn was demanding, as he held him in a steel-strong grip, 'Barron, damn you, have you gone mad? That's going to rouse the countryside! If you were a Darkovan, you'd be hanged on the spot for raising a false fear!'

'False fear be – – ' he swore atrociously. 'The Ghost Wind! I smelled it! By night it will be everywhere!'

His face slowly blanching, Colryn stared at him. 'The Ghost Wind? How do you know?'

'I smelled it, I tell you! What do you do here to rouse the countryside for taking shelter?'

Colryn looked at him, only half believing but gripped by his obvious sincerity. 'The beacon will alert them,' he said, 'and I can signal with the mirror, after which they will ring bells in the villages. We have a good alarm system here. I still think you're insane. I don't smell it at all, but then for all I know you could have a better nose than mine. And I won't take a chance on letting the Ghost Wind—or the Ya-men — get anyone.' He shoved Barron out of his way. 'Look where you're going! Damn it, what's the matter, are you *blind*? You'll be in the ditch in a minute!' He forgot Barron again, and ran toward the station for the signaling device. Eyes closed, Barron stood listening to the beacon crackle. He was aware of the pungency of the burning beacon and through it, the growing, sick scent of the pollen-laden Ghost Wind blowing from the heights.

After a while, still disoriented, he turned and made his way, on faltering feet, inside the station. Colryn was on the tower, signaling. Paradoxically, the thing which surprised Barron most was that he was not surprised at himself; he had a vague sense of split selfhood, in the same sort of divided, underwater consciousness that he had felt once or twice before.

The next hour was insane confusion: shouts and voices, bells beginning to ring in the villages below, and the rangers at the station running about on errands they didn't bother explaining. He kept his eyes closed against further disorientation and kept out of the way. It seemed natural to sit by while others acted; he had done his part. Presently men came riding up the slope in crazy haste and he became aware that Larry had come in and was standing with Colryn in front of him.

'What happened?'

'He smelled the Ghost Wind,' Colryn said tersely.

'And in good time,' Larry said. 'Thank the gods we have warning. I had just barely begun to wonder if I smelled it myself when I heard the bells and ordered everyone back — but it's still so faint I can hardly make it out! How did you know?' he demanded. Barron did not answer, but only shook his head. After a little while Larry went away.

He thought, *I have done a foolish thing; before, he only suspected something strange, but now he will know, and if he does not, Valdir will. Valdir is Comyn and he will know exactly what has happened.*

I don't care what they do to the Earthman, but I must get away. I should have kept quiet and escaped in the confusion of the Ghost Wind.

But I couldn't let them all go through that danger; and Lerrys would have been caught on the hills. I owe him something. There is a blade between us.

Nothing human will dare to move in these mountains tonight. I must lie low and keep from attracting any more attention to Barron until then.

And then — then I must be gone, long gone, before Valdir comes!

——— 8 ———

It seemed eternities that he watchfully waited, that curious doubled consciousness keeping him nerve-strained, but holding himself back from being noticed. He kept out of the way while the men at the station hurried around, making all secure as the wind rose higher, screaming around the corners of the station and the fire tower. The sickish smell grew stronger by the moment and he fancied he could feel it penetrating to the rest of his nose, into the brain, subtly eating away at his humanity and his resolution.

Nor were the others unaffected; at one point Colryn stopped in his work of nailing heavy shutters tight and bent over, crouching, his arms wrapped round his head as if in terrible pain. He began a low, crazy moaning. Gwynn, hurrying through the room on some errand or other, saw him there, went to him, knelt beside him, put an arm around his shoulders and talked to him in a low, reassuring voice, until Colryn shook his head violently as if to clear it of something. Then he stood up and swung his arms, swore, thanked Gwynn and went on with his work.

The man who was not sure at the moment whether he was Dan Barron or someone else, stayed where he was, fighting for self-control; but he was not unaffected. As the wind rose and the smell of the Ghost Wind grew stronger, strange images spun in his mind – primordial memories laden with fear and terror – frightening hungers. Once he jerked upright from a waking nightmare of kneeling over a prone man, tearing at his throat with his teeth. He shuddered, rose and began to walk feverishly around the room.

When all was secure they sat down to food, but no one ate much. They were all silent, all tormented by the rising scream of the wind, which tore at their ears and their nerves, and by the spinning of vague hallucinatory images in their eyes and their minds. Barron kept his eyes closed. It seemed easier to eat that way, without the unfamiliar distraction of sight.

Halfway through the meal, the faraway shrieking began; a high, keening, space-filling howl and yelp that rose higher and higher, through the audible frequencies, and seemed to go on even after it could be heard no more.

'Ya-men,' said Gwynn tersely, and let his knife drop to the table with a clatter.

'They can't get into the station,' Colryn said, but he didn't sound sure. No one after that made much more than a pretense at eating, and before long they left the food and dishes uncleared on the table and went into the shuttered and barricaded main room of the station. The yelping and howling went on – at first distant and intermittent, then constant and close. Eyes closed, Barron saw in his mind's eye a ring of towering plumed forms, raging and shrieking and hurling themselves, in a maddened dance, around the peak of the hill.

Once Colryn tried to drown out the sound by beginning a song; but his voice died away, halfway through the first verse.

The night wore on. Toward the deepest part of the darkness, the pounding and banging began; it sounded as if a heavy form hurled itself, again and again, against the barred doors, and fell back, howling with bruised, insensate rage. Once begun, it went on and on, until their nerves were screaming.

Once Larry said low in the darkness, 'I wonder what they're really like? It seems hell that the only time they come out of the deep woods, they're maddened – and we can't communicate with them.'

Gwynn said, with bleak humor, 'I'll unbar the door, if you want to try a little nonhuman diplomacy.'

Larry shuddered and was still. Colryn said, 'Upstairs in

the lens–grinding room there's a glass window. We should get a look at them from there.'

Gwynn refused, with a shudder, and so did the other rangers; but Colryn, Larry and Barron went up the stairs together. It was something to do. At this height, the window had not been covered or barricaded. They did not light the lamp, knowing the light would attract the howling nonhumans outside. They went to the glass and, cupping their hands around their eyes, peered through.

Outside, though he had expected it to be dark and stormy, it was clear moonlight – one of the rare nights on Darkover when rain and fog had not blotted out the moons. The air seemed filled with swirling dust, through which he saw the Ya–men.

They were hugely tall, nine feet at least, and looked like tall emaciated men, wearing plumed head–dresses, until he saw their faces. They had huge heads and terrible beaked faces like strange birds of prey, and they moved with a clumsy swiftness that was like the wind–tossed branches of the trees which dipped and surged at the edge of the clearing. There were at least three dozen of them, it seemed, and perhaps more. After a little, as if by common consent, the men turned away from the window and went down the stairs again.

Barron, about to follow them, remained behind. The strangeness was growing in him again. Something turning like a thermostat in his brain told him that the tide of the Ghost Wind had turned. There was no change in the slamming noise of the wind, nor in the howling of the nonhumans, but he *knew*.

They will be gone long before dawn. The wind will die and there will be rain. Only the mad and the desperate travel on Darkover by night, but I – perhaps I am both desperate and mad.

An enormous crash, and cries from downstairs, told him that the slamming attack of the nonhumans had crashed an outbuilding. He did not go down to investigate; it was not his affair. Silently, moving like an automation, he went in the darkness to the chest of drawers where he kept his clothing. He discarded the thin indoor garments he was wearing, put on leather riding breeches, a thick woven shirt and a heavy tunic. He slipped into Colryn's room and appropriated the man's heavy, fur-lined cloak. He had a long way to ride and a cloak was better than a jacket. He regretted that he must steal a horse, but if he lived, it would be returned or paid for, and if not, he reminded himself of the mountain proverb, 'when Eternity comes all will be understood and forgiven.'

He cocked a practiced ear; the wind was definitely quieting. In another hour the Ya-men would be gone, the restless impulse that had led them there entirely gone; they would waken to terror and strangeness and creep timidly back to their caves and nests in the deepest woods. *The poor devils must feel damn near as strange as I do.*

The slamming of the wind was subsiding and even in the incessant howling there were gaps now, intervals grew wider and finally lessened to nothing. Peering through the glass, he saw that the clearing was empty. Not more than half an hour after that, he heard the other men coming up to the large room where they slept. Someone called, 'Barron, are you all right?' He froze, then made himself answer in a sleepy, resentful mutter.

In a few more minutes a silence lay over the fire station, broken only by the snores of exhausted men in the far room, and the rattle of occasional branches in the dying wind. Peering through the glass, he saw that fog was rising. There would be rain and it would lay the last traces of the poison from the Ghost Wind.

All was quiet, but nevertheless he waited another hour, to dispel the chance that one of the men, sleeping lightly after fear and tension, would waken and hear him. Then, moving with infinite caution so that the stairs would not creak beneath him, he stole downstairs. He made up a parcel of food from the leavings on the table. They had left the doors barricaded, but it was no great trouble to unfasten the bars and take them down.

He was outside in the bitter cold and fading moonlight of the mountain night.

He had to find a clawed tool to unfasten the bars they

had nailed over the door of the stable, and in order to use it, confused by its unfamiliar weight in his hand, he had to close his eyes and let the inner reflexes take over. He thanked his fate that the stable was at some distance from the house, otherwise the racket he made as he wrestled with the heavy boards would certainly have wakened even such weary sleepers, and they would have come down raising an outcry against thieves. He got them loose and stole inside.

The stable was warm, dark and friendly-familiar with the smell of horses. He shut his eyes to saddle up the horse; it was easier to handle the harness that way. The beast recognized him and neighed softly and he began to talk to it soothingly in an undertone. 'Yes, fellow, we have a long ride tonight, but quiet, do you hear? We must get away quietly. Not used to going in the dark, are you? Well, I am, so don't you worry about that.'

He dared not mount and ride till at some distance. Taking the bridle, he led the horse carefully down the slope and down the mountain road, then paused to take stock. He was ready; he closed his eyes to orient himself. He must go over the ranges and past the castle he could see from the fire tower, skirt the bends of the River Kadarin and beware of trailmen in the forested slopes on the near side. Then the road toward Carthon lay clear before him.

He was warmly clad. He had a good horse; it was Gwynn's, which was the best, one of the finely bred blacks which the Altons bred for the rangers. He had heard Gwynn boast that Valdir had broken this one with his own hands. It was a crime to deprive the ranger of such a beauty; yet – Necessity would make a thief even of a Hastur,' he reminded himself grimly. Yet another proverb came to mind: 'If you're going to steal horses, steal thoroughbreds.'

He was well provided with money. Nudged by his subtle prodding, Barron had had Valdir change his Terran credits for Darkovan coins.

He spared a thought for Barron. It was almost a pity to do this to the Earthman, but he had had no choice. One of the greatest of crimes on Darkover, ever since the days of the Compact, was to take over another human mind. It could only be done with another latent telepath, and telepaths on Darkover were aware, and they guarded against such invasion. He had hoped to find an idiot mind, so that he would be robbing no man of his own soul. But instead, as his mind ranged in the desperation of trance, unbound by the limitations of space, he had touched Barron . . .

Were the Terrans even human? In any case, what did it matter what happened to these invaders on our world. Barron is an intruder, an outsider – fair game.

And what could I do, blind and helpless, but this?

At the foot of the path leading to the fire station, he came to a halt and swung into the saddle. He was on his way.

And for a bare instant Dan Barron, confused, disoriented, surfaced as if coming up from a long, deep dive. Was this another hallucination – that he was riding along a dark road, faint dying moonlight overhead, icy wind whistling around his shoulders? No, this was real – where was he going? And why? He shuddered in terror, jerking on the horse's reins . . .

He disappeared again into fathomless darkness.

The man in the saddle urged his horse to top speed: by dawn he wished to be hidden from the station by hills, so that when he emerged again, if they sought him from there he would simply be another man on horseback, moving on his lawful occasions through the countryside. He was very weary, but as if he had taken some euphoric drug, not at all sleepy. For the first time in his sheltered, invalid's life he was not resting inert, waiting for someone else to take action. He was going to do this himself.

He had stopped briefly three times to let his horse rest and breathe before the great red rim of the sun peered over the hills. He found a sheltered clearing and hobbled the horse. He rolled himself in his blanket and slept for an hour, then rose, ate a little cold food from his saddlebag and was on his way again.

All that day he rode through the hills, keeping to little-known roads – if Larry had sent for Valdir the one thing he did not dare was to meet Valdir on the road. Valdir had the old Comyn powers, which made his own look feeble by contrast. Valdir would know at once what he had done. The Storns had no traffic with the Comyn; certainly they would not come to his aid, even in this emergency. He must keep clear of the Comyn.

Toward noon it became cloudy, and Storn, looking up, saw gray caps hanging over the far hills. He thought of Melitta making her way toward Carthon from the far side of the Kadarin, and wondered, despairingly, if she could make her way across the passes in time. Snow must be falling on the heights; and in the hills there were bandits, trailmen, and the terrible banshee birds, which hunted anything living and could disembowel man or horse with one stroke of their terrible claws. He could do nothing to help Melitta now; he could help them both best by bringing himself safe to Carthon.

All that day he met no one on the road except an occasional farmer working in his fields, or, in scattered villages, miles apart, women chatting in the streets with rosy children clustered around them. None of them paid attention to him, except in one village where he stopped to ask a woman selling fruit by the road for a drink of water from her well; he bought some fruit, and two small boys sidled up to admire the horse and ask, shyly, if it was the Alton breed, which gave him a moment's shock.

A Storn of Storn, fugitive and thief!

He slept again in the woods, rolled in his cloak. Towards afternoon of the second day he heard hoofbeats on the road, far off, ahead of him. Riding after, hanging at a distance lest he be seen and the horse, perhaps, recognized by the wrong people, he found that the small road he was travelling spread out into a wide, graveled surface, almost a highway. He must be nearing the Kadarin. Now he could see the riders ahead of him. They were a long line of men wearing cloaks of unfamiliar cut and color – tall men, sandy-haired, fair, and fierce-looking. Only a few of them and horses; the others rode the antlered, heavy-set pack beasts. He recognized them – Dry-towners from

Shainsa or Daillon returning home after trading in the mountains. They would not recognize him and they would have no interest in him, but, as was customary in these lands, they would let him travel in their company for a small fee, since everyone added to their band was an extra protection against bandits or nonhuman attackers.

He spurred his horse and rode after them, already rehearsing what he would say. He was Storn of Storn Heights, a man who need fear nothing in foothills or mountains.

He could ride with them almost as far as Carthon.

He was safe now. He prayed, with gut-wrenching intensity, that Melitta had had equal luck – that she, too, was safe. He dared not let his mind range backward to Storn Heights, to the castle where his body lay entranced behind the blue fire, guarded by magnetic fields; that might draw him back. He dared not think of Allira, brought to a bandit's bed, or to Edric, wounded and alone in the dungeons of his own castle.

He sent his hail ringing out after the caravan and saw the riders stop.

—— 9 ——

They rode down into Carthon at midmorning, as the morning mist was beginning to burn away under the quick, hot sun.

For five days they had ridden through diminishing mountains and foothills and now they came between the hills into the wide plain which lay in the bend of the River Kadarin – where Carthon lay bleaching on the plains. It had the look of incredible age; the squat buildings were like mountains leveled by the erosion of millennia. It was the first part of Darkover that he had seen where there were no trees. The Dry-towners had been silent and apprehensive moving through the mountainous forests; but now, with the ancient city lying in their gaze, they cheered visibly. Even their pack animals quickened their steps, and one of the men began to sing a heptatonic melody in a rough and guttural dialect that Storn could not understand.

For Storn – despite his fear of being overtaken, the constant and growing sense that he was pursued, and his endless apprehension for Melitta, struggling somewhere in the snows and passes around High Kimbi – the journey had been magical. For the first time in his life he tasted freedom and even adventure; he was treated as a man among men, not as a handicapped invalid. Deliberately he had suspended his fears for his sister, the thought of Edric and Allira in danger and captivity, and his own sense of guilt for breaking one of the most rigid of Darkovan taboos – the meddling with another human soul. He dared not think about these things; if he let his mind roam back or forward, he risked losing control of the man he had mastered; once, in fact, in the night while Storn dreamed, Barron had wakened in astonishment and terror, looking around at the unfamiliar surroundings and ready to panic and run wild. Only with difficulty had Storn resumed the upper hand. He could feel somewhere, at a level beyond his control – in that ultimate fastness of the human spirit where not even a telepath or Keeper could penetrate – Barron watched and defied him. But Storn kept control. He told himself now that even for Barron's sake he must maintain surface control – among Dry-towners, a Terran would not be permitted to live. Small was the contact between Terran and Darkovan in valley and mountain country; with the Dry towns it was absolutely minimal. Many of them had never seen or heard of the Terran Empire cities, and in the Dry towns any stranger walked with his life in his hands. An off-worlder could not have maintained safety for a single day.

As they reached Carthon, Storn realized that his single-minded enjoyment of the journey was of necessity coming to an end. Carthon had been deserted years ago by the valley lords, who had withdrawn into the mountains when the fertility of the land failed and the river changed its course. It had become a no-man's-land, inhabited by the flotsam and jetsam of a dozen civilizations. At one time, Storn remembered – he had travelled here twice in his boyhood, with his late father, long before assuming the heirship of his house – it had been the haunt of half a dozen bands of mercenaries, recruited from mountain bandits, renegade Dry-towners and the gods alone knew what else. It had been Storn's thought that here he might hire one of these bands to aid in freeing High Windward. It would not be easy – Brynat had had no easy task and a captain of that quality would not be simply dislodged – but Storn knew a trick or two, besides knowing every niche of the castle. With an able band of mercenary soldiers he had no doubt of his ability to recapture his home.

He had urged Melitta to meet him there because he was, or had been at that time, uncertain of the ultimate degree of control he could establish over Barron. He could have sent her alone, keeping only telepathic contact with her; but he was not sure of her continuing ability to maintain rapport over long periods of time and distance. What Storn knew of the old Darkovan *laran* powers was of necessity incomplete and based on trial and error. Only the long, idle childhood and adolescence of a man born blind had given him leisure and impetus to explore them, and he had had no teacher. They had been a way to alleviate his terrible boredom and the feeling of worthlessness felt by a physically handicapped man in a society which put great reliance on strength, physical skill and action. He knew that he had accomplished a great deal for a man with his handicap, even in the fields proper to a man of his family and caste: he could ride; he could climb skillfully in his own mountain cliffs and crags with little help; and he administered his own estates, with his sisters and young brother at his side. In fact, not the least of his pride was in that he had won, and kept, the loyalty of his younger brother in a society where brothers were often bitter rivals and he could easily have been relegated to the background, with Edric taking his place as Lord of Storn. To them – until Brynat had appeared and made war – he had seemed strong and competent. Only when the castle was under siege had he tasted the bitterness of helplessness.

But now the other things he had explored were coming into their own. His body was guarded against Brynat, and he was free to seek help and revenge – if he could get it.

The red sun was high and warm, and he had thrown back his riding cloak when they rode through the gates of Carthon. At first glance he could see that it was unlike any of the mountain villages they had ridden through; it felt, sounded and smelled like no Darkovan city he had ever know. The very air was different; it smelled of spice, incense and dust. It was obvious to Storn that in the intervening years more and more Dry-towners had moved into Carthon, possibly in search of the more abundant water from the Kadarin River, or perhaps – the thought crossed his mind – feeling that the lowlands' and valleys' peaceful peoples would lie there at their mercy. He dismissed the thought for later worry.

Nevertheless he felt apprehensive. He was less confident in his ability to win help in a predominantly Dry-town area. Traditionally they had their own concerns and their own culture, he could offend them fatally by a chance word. From what he had heard and what he had seen travelling with these merchants in the last days, their prime motivation was the scoring of points in an elaborate, never-ending game of prestige. No outsider could hope to win anything in this game, and Storn, travelling in their company, had been ignored, as men intent on a gambling game will ignore the cat by the fireplace.

It was humiliating, but he knew it was safer that way. He had no knowledge and no skill in knife fights, and they lived by an elaborate dueling code under which the man who could not defend himself to the death against enemy or friend was dead.

It was a forlorn hope that he could find Dry-towner mercenaries here. Still, there might be mountain or valley bands here, even though the predominant culture now seemed Dry-town. And even Dry-towners might be tempted by the thought of sacking Brynat's riches. He was prepared to offer them all the loot of Brynat and his men. All he wanted was the freedom of Storn Castle and peace to enjoy it.

They had passed the city gates, giving their names at the outworks to fierce-looking, bearded men; Storn saw with relief that some of them wore familiar mountain garments and heard them speaking a dialect of his own language. Perhaps they were not all Dry-towners here. The city was wide-flung, not like the huddled mountain villages cramped behind protective walls or the *forsts*, the forest forts behind high stockades. The outworks seemed little manned. Everywhere were the tall, fair-haired Dry-town men, and women walked in the open dusty streets – slender Dry-town women, sun-burnt and swift, carrying their heads proudly and moving in the tiny chiming sound of chains, the jewelled fetters that bound their hands, restricted movement and that proclaimed them chattel to some man of power and wealth.

At the main square of the city the caravan turned purposely toward the Eastern quarter, and Storn was reminded that their agreement terminated here. Now he was on his own – alone, in a culture and country strange to him, where any moment might bring some fatal blunder. But before he began to rack his brains as to how he could best explore the possibilities, the leader of the caravan turned back and said bluntly, 'Stranger; be reminded that in our towns all strangers must first pay respects at the Great House. The Lord Rannath will be better disposed toward you if you come of your free will in courtesy, than if his men must hail you here to give an account of yourself.'

'For this my thanks.' Storn gave the formal return and thought that these Dry-town newcomers had indeed moved into Carthon in quantity; nothing like this had obtained when he came there as a boy. The bitter thought crossed his mind that this Lord Rannath, whoever he might be, had no doubt moved into Carthon much as Brynat had moved into Storn Castle, and with as much authority.

It was nothing to him who ruled in Carthon. And in the Great House he might learn what he wanted to know.

In Carthon all roads led to the central plaza of the city. There was no mistaking the Great House, a vast structure of curiously opalescent stone lying at the center of the main plaza. Low, dusty beds ·of flowers grew in great profusion in the outer courts, and the Dry-town men and women came and went through the halls as if moving in a formal dance. The women, safe and insolent behind the protection of the chains, cast him sidelong smiles and bright-eyed glances, and murmured phrases he could not well understand. Only the repeated murmur of *charrat* was familiar; it was another form of *chaireth*, stranger. *Stranger indeed*, he thought with a flash of unaccustomed self-pity. *Doubly and trebly stranger, and just now without even the time and freedom to answer these bold looks* . . .

He had expected to be stopped somewhere and asked his business, but evidently formal manners either did not exist here or were so alien that he did not recognize them as such. Following the shifting crowds he finally came into the main hall, and realized that it was evidently the hour for audience.

Elegance and a bleak luxury there was, but it was barren and alien here; this room was meant for rich hangings and the luxurious furniture of valley nobility. Stripped to the bare Dry-town manner it seemed as if it had been looted; the windows were bare, letting in harsh light, and there were no furnishings apart from low pallets and a great central thronelike chair on which lay a crown and sword, with hieratic formality in their arrangement on the gold cushion. The throne was empty. A young man, his chin just fuzzed with blond beard too sparse for shaving sat on a pallet beside the throne. He wore a fur shirt cloak and high, exquisitely dyed and embroidered leather boots. As Storn approached him, he looked up and said, 'I am the voice of the Lord Rannath; I am called Kerstal. My house is the house of Greystone. Have you feud or sworn blood with me or against me?'

Storn desperately mustered what little he knew of Dry-town customs. He started to answer in the formal and stilted Cahuenga tongue, *lingua franca* of Darkover between mountain and valley, Dry-town and river folk, then suddenly dropped the pretense. He said, drawing a deep breath and stiffening his backbone, 'Not to the best of my knowledge, no; to the best of my knowledge I never heard of your house and, therefore, I have never offended against it, contracted debts to it, nor do they owe me anything. I come here as a stranger, strange to your customs; if I offend against them, it is done unwittingly and seeking peace. On my last visit to Carthon the Great House was vacant; I offer such respects as a stranger should – no more and no less. If other courtesy is required, I request that you tell me.'

There was a little chiming of chains as the women in the hall turned toward him, and a small breath of surprise ran all around the room. Kerstal seemed very briefly taken aback by the unaccustomed answer. Then he said, with a brief nodding of his head, 'Bravely spoken and no offense given or taken. Yet none walk in Carthon without leave of the Lord Rannath and his House. Who is your liege lord and what business brings you here?'

'As for my liege, I am a free man of the mountains, with fealty sworn to none,' Storn returned proudly. 'I am my own man, and in my own place men give me loyalty at their own will, not from constraint.' It flashed over him that pride would serve him better here than any other commodity. Dry-towners seemed to respect arrogance; if he came as a suppliant, they might kick him out without listening. 'My house is the house of High Windward, in the Domain of the Aldarans, ancient lords of the Comyn. As for my business here, it is not with you; does your custom require that I must make it known? In my place, a questioner must show that his question is neither idle curiosity nor prying malice; if it is otherwise here, show me reason to respect your customs, and I will do so.'

Again the little ripple of surprise ran round the room and Kerstal moved to lay his hand on the hilt of the sword which lay on the vacant throne, then paused. He rose to his feet, and now his voice had courtesy rather than negligence. He said, 'In the absence of sworn blood feud between us, then, *Charrat* of the house of Storn, be welcome to Carthon. No law requires that you make your affairs known, if they are your own – yet a question locked behind your lips will be forever unanswered. Tell me what you seek in Carthon, and if I can honorably answer, it will be my pleasure to do so.' A faint smile touched his face, and Storn relaxed, knowing he had won. Dry-towners valued control above all else; if a Dry-towner relaxed enough to smile, you were probably safe with him.

Storn said, 'My ancestral house has been attacked and laid under siege by a bandit known as Brynat Scarface; I seek men and aid to redeem my house's strength, honor and integrity.' He used the word *kihar*, that untranslatable idiom for face, personal integrity and honor. 'My kinsmen and the women of our people are at their mercy.'

Kerstal frowned faintly. 'And you are here, alive and unwounded?'

'Dead men have no *kihar*,' Storn answered swiftly. 'Nor can the dead come to the aid of kinsmen.'

Kerstal paused to consider this. Behind them, in the outer hallways, there was a stir and an outcry, and some vague familiar sound in that cry touched every nerve in Storn to immediate response. He could not identify it, but something was happening out there . . .

But Kerstal paid the noises no heed. He said slowly, 'There is some justice in that, stranger of Storn, and – your ways are not ours – no ineradicable loss of honor. Nevertheless, our people will not, I warn you, become entangled in mountain feuds. The House of Rannath does not sell their swords in the mountains; there is enough *kihar* to be found on our own plains.'

'Nor have I asked it of you,' Storn replied quickly. 'When last I visited Carthon there were many who were willing to sell their swords for the chance of reward. I ask only freedom to seek them.'

'Freedom of that sort cannot be denied you,' Kerstal replied,' and if your tale is true, the House of Rannath will not forbid any free and unsworn man to give you his service. Speak then your name, *charrat* of Storn.'

Storn drew himself up to his full height.

'I bear my father's name, with pride,' he said, and his voice, although it sounded strange to himself, rang loud and clear – a strong bass voice – through that hall. 'I am Loran Rakhal Storn, Lord of Storn, of High Windward.'

Kerstal looked at him flatly and unreadably and said, 'You lie.'

And all around the hall, another sound ran; Storn had never heard it before, but nevertheless, he could not be mistaken. All around the hall, men were drawing their swords. He cast one quick look around.

He stood in a ring of naked blades.

─── 10 ───

Melitta had stopped struggling now. She walked between her captors, her head down, thinking bitterly, *I've failed. It wasn't enough to fight my way across the passes, hiding from banshee birds at night, getting lost in the snow, the horse freezing to death in the heights . . . No, I manage to get all the way to Carthon and the first thing that happens is, I'm grabbed up as soon as I walk into the city!*

Think Melitta, think — there must be a way. What do they want with you, what law have you broken? Storn would never have sent you here if it was impossible for you to find help. But did Storn know?

She drew herself up to her full height, wrenching herself to a stop between the tall, fair-haired men. 'I will not go another step before I am told what is my offense,' she said. 'I am a free woman of the mountains, and I know nothing of your laws.'

One of the men said briefly 'Masterless wenches' — the word he used was untranslatable into Melitta's own language, but she had heard it used as a particularly filthy insult — 'do not walk free here in Carthon among decent people, no matter what your custom may be beyond the Kadarin.'

'Have you no courtesy for the customs of strangers?' she demanded.

'For customs in common decency,' said one — the dialect so thick and barbarous that she had trouble understanding — 'but every woman who comes here must be properly owned and controlled, and her master known. It is for the Lord of Rannath to say what shall be done with you, wench.'

Melitta relaxed her taut muscles and let herself be drawn along, among staring men and the soft laughter of the women. She saw their chained hands with something like horror, and was shamed for them and astonished that they could hold up their heads and walk with something that looked like pride. Seeing their robes and their fair hair bound with ribbons and jewels she was more than ever conscious of her travel-worn riding cloak, the patched and faded breeches she wore – even the relatively free manners of mountain girls on Darkover did not accept breeches for riding, and only desperation had driven Melitta to wear them – and her hair, damp with sweat and dirty and straggling with the dust of the road. She flushed dull red. It was no miracle indeed if they thought her the lowest of the low. She wanted to cry.

Lady of Storn, she thought. *Yes, damn it, don't I just look like it!*

They were going through a bare archway now and she saw men and women gathered in a ring around a throne where a standing man, one of the fair-haired Dry-towners but taller and better dressed than most, was questioning a man in mountain clothing. Her captors said, 'The Voice of Rannath is not at leisure; wait here, wench.' They relaxed their grip.

Melitta's command of Cahuenga was not very fluent, and she stood without listening, trying to recover her own self-possession and glad of the respite. What could she say to convince the lords of this city that she was a free and responsible human being and not a chattel to come under their stupid laws about women? Perhaps she should have sought help in the foothills. The Comyn lords at Armida and at Castle Ardais were no kin to her family but they might have shown her hospitality and then she could have proceeded to Carthon dressed as befitted her rank, and properly escorted. She had heard that the lord Valdir Alton was a wise and enlightened man who had done much to safeguard his own people against the raids of mountain bandits and had led an expedition to root out the *forst* of the notorious Cyrillon des Trailles. Everyone in the

Kilghard hills, Storns included, had slept safer in their beds after that. *Certainly he would have been willing to come to our aid against Brynat,* she thought.

She was not trying to follow the conversation between the man her captors had styled the Voice of Rannath and his prisoner, but the prisoner caught her attention. He was unusually tall, with reddish-dark hair and a heavy and sombre face, with something strange about his expression and eyes. She wished she could see him more clearly and understand his words. She could see that he was making some impression on the Voice of Rannath, for the Dry-towner was smiling. Then, before Melitta's electrified ears, the very voice and accent of her brother rang through the hall, drawing her upright in a frenzy of bewilderment.

'I am Loran Rakhal Storn, Lord of Storn, of High Wind-ward!'

Melitta stifled a cry. It had evidently been the wrong thing for him to say; the smile was gone from Kerstal's face. He rapped out something and suddenly every man in the room had drawn his knife and they were closing in on the unlucky stranger at the center of the circle.

Kerstal said, 'You lie. You lie, stranger. The son of Storn is not personally known to me; but his father is known to mine, and the men of Storn are known to our house. Shall I tell you how you lie? Storn men are fair-haired; the eyes of Storn men are gray. And it is known to me, as it is known to every man from the Hellers to Thendara, that the Lord of Storn has been blind from birth – blind beyond cure! Now state your true name, liar and braggart, or run the gauntlet to save your wretched skin!'

And suddenly, with a gasp of horror, Melitta understood. She understood what Storn had done – and quailed, for a thing that was a crime beyond words – and why he had done it, and what she must do to save them both.

'Let me through,' she said, her voice clear and high. 'He lies not. No Storn of Storn lies, and when my words are heard let any who belies us call challenge on either or both. I am Melitta of Storn, and if the House of Storn is known to you, father and son, then look in my face and read *my* lineage there.'

Shaking off the hands of the startled men who held her, she made her way forward. The closed ring of knife-wielding Dry-towners parted before her and closed after her. She heard a rippling whisper of wonder run round the circle. Someone said, 'Is this some Free Amazon of the lowlands, that she walks shameless and unchained? Women of the Comyn Domains are shamefast and modest; how came this maid here?'

'I am no Free Amazon but a woman of the mountains,' said Melitta, facing the speaker. 'Storn is my name and Storn is my household.'

Kerstal turned toward her. He stared at her for some minutes; then his hand fell from his knife hilt, and he bent in the formal bow of the Dry-towners, his hands spread briefly.

'Lady of Storn; your heritage speaks in your face. Your father's daughter is welcome here. But who is this braggart who calls kin with you? Do you claim *him* as kin?'

Melitta walked toward the stranger. Her mind was racing. She said quickly, in the mountain tongue, 'Storn, is it you? Loran, why did you do it?'

'I had no choice,' he replied. 'It was the only way to save you all.'

'Tell me quickly the name of the horse I first learned to ride, and I accept you for who you are.'

A faint flicker of a smile passed over the stranger's face. 'You did not learn to ride on a horse, but on a stag pony,' he said softly, 'and you called him *Horny-pig*.'

Deliberately Melitta went to the stranger's side, laid her hand in his and stood on tiptoe to kiss his cheek. 'Kinsman,' she said slowly, and turned back to Kerstal.

'Kinsman of mine he is indeed,' she said. 'Nor did he lie when he named himself Storn of Storn. Our mountain ways are unknown to you. My brother of Storn is, as you say, blind beyond cure and thus unable to hold *laran* right in our house; and thus this cousin of ours, adopted into our

109

household, wears the name and title of Storn, his true name forgotten even by brother and sister, *nedestro* heir to Storn.'

For a moment after she spoke the words she held her breath; then, at a signal from Kerstal, the knives dropped. Melitta dared not let her face show relief.

Storn spoke softly: 'What redress does the Great House of Rannath give for deadly insult?'

'I am the Voice of Rannath only,' Kerstal countered. 'Learn our customs another time, stranger.'

'It seems to me,' Storn said, his voice still gentle, 'that Storns have suffered grave ills at your hands. Deadly insult given to me, and my sister – ' His eyes turned on the two men who had haled Melitta into the Hall. 'Is this your courtesy to strangers in your city?'

'Amends shall be made,' Kerstal said. Beads of sweat stood out on his forehead. 'My House has no quarrel with you, Lord of Storn; be then our guests and receive gifts consonant with your quality. Let the exchange of courtesy wipe out memory of offense given or taken.'

Stern hesitated, his hand on the hilt of his knife, and Melitta, reading the gesture with astonishment, thought, *He's enjoying this; he half hopes that Kerstal will call challenge!*

But if this was Storn's intention, he remembered his primary intention in time. He said, 'Be it so, then. My sister and I gratefully accept your hospitality, kinsman of Rannath,' and all round the circle, there were small sighs and stirs of relief or, perhaps, of disappointment.

Kerstal summoned servants and gave orders, then detained Storn a moment with a raised hand. 'You claim this woman, then? See you to it that she does not walk abroad free in defiance of our customs!'

Melitta bit her tongue on an angry retort, feeling Storn's hand dig hard into her shoulder. This was no time to start any further arguments.

A few minutes later, they were in a large guest room, bare as all Dry-town rooms, with little more than mats on the floor and a shelf or two. When the servants had withdrawn, Melitta faced the stranger who bore her brother's voice and manner. Left alone with him, she hardly knew what to say.

The stranger said softly, in their own language, 'It's really me, you know, Melitta.' He smiled. 'I must say – you came at exactly the right moment. We couldn't have planned it better!'

'No planning of mine, but good luck,' she conceded. She sank down wearily. 'Why did you send me here?'

'Because at one time there were mountain-born mercenaries all through this part of the country, gathering at Carthon. Now, with the Dry-towners moving in here, I'm not sure,' Storn said. 'But we are free; we can act. We could do nothing, now, at High Windward.' He threw himself down on one of the pallets. Melitta too, was tired beyond words and she was also ill at ease with a man who still seemed a stranger to her. At last she said, 'Who is – the man – '

'His name is Barron; he is a Terran, an off-worlder. His mind lay open to me; I scanned his future and saw that he would be coming into the mountains. And so –' Storn shrugged. Another of those silences fell between brother and sister, a silence which could not be talked about. They both knew that Storn had broken an ancient taboo, forbidden from the earliest years of the Darkovan Compact. Even though the victim was a Terran, the horror remained with Melitta.

They were both relieved when servants of Rannath entered, bearing trays of food, and a pair of chests which, the servants explained, were gifts from the House of Rannath to the Lord and Lady of Storn. When they had gone away again, Melitta rose and approached the pile of gifts, and Storn laughed softly. 'Never too tired to be curious – just like a woman! As a matter of fact, Melitta, enjoy these gifts with clear conscience – Rannath's Voice, or whatever that official calls himself, knows that he is purchasing immunity from a blood feud that would run for years and cost him a hell of a lot more than this! If we were Dry-towners, that is. He'll despise us a little because we can be bought off, but I for one don't care a scrap for what a patch of unwashed Dry-towners think about us, do you? I accepted the gifts because, among other things' – he surveyed her – 'you looked as if you could use a few gifts! I've never seen you look so hoydenish, little sister!'

Melitta felt ready to cry. 'You don't know half of where I've been, or how I've had to travel, and you're making fun of what I'm wearing – ' Her voice broke.

'Melitta! Don't cry, don't – ' He reached out and took her into his arms, holding her tight, her face on his shoulder. 'Little sister, *breda, chiya* . . . ' He cuddled her, crooning pet names from their childhood. Gradually she quieted, then drew away, vaguely embarrassed. The voice, the manner, were her brother's, but the strange man's body and touch were disconcerting. She lowered her eyes, and Storn laughed, embarrassed.

'Let's see what Kerstal has sent us, and we'll see how high he rates the *kihar* of the House of Storn.'

'Not cheaply, at any rate,' Melitta said, opening the chests.

There was a sword of fine temper for Storn. He buckled it on, saying, 'Remember, these are Dry-towners – it does not mean what it would mean in our mountains. Worse luck, or it would be a pledge to come to our aid.' With the sword was an embroidered vest and baldric. For Melitta, as she had hoped, were gowns of linen trimmed with fur, hoods and coifs – and a gilt chain with a tiny padlock. She stared at that, unbelieving.

Storn laughed as he picked it up: 'Evidently he thinks I'm going to put you on a leash!' Then, as her eyes flashed again, he added quickly, 'Never mind, you don't have to wear it. Come, *breda*, let us eat, and then rest for a little while. We're safe here, at least. Time enough tomorrow to think about what we're going to do, if Rannath decides that no one here can help us.'

Storn had proved an accurate prophet. However eager the House of Rannath might be to avoid a lengthy blood feud with the Storns, the word had evidently gone out all over Carthon; no one was 'at leisure,' as he told them regretfully, to pursue a war in the mountains.

Storn, privately, didn't blame them. The Dry-towners were never at ease in the foothills, let alone in the high passes; and the House of Rannath had enough to do to hold Carthon, without scattering such armies as he could command on missions in the far Sierras. For that matter, Dry-town mercenaries, unskilled at mountaineering and ill-guarded against snow and cold, would be more trouble than they were worth. They needed mountain men, and there were none in Carthon.

When the brother and sister insisted on taking their leave, Kerstal besought them to stay and managed not to sound nearly as insincere as they both knew he was. When they pleaded urgent necessity, he found Melitta an excellent riding horse from his private stables and pressed it upon her as a gift.

'And thus,' Storn said cynically as they rode away from the Great House, 'the Voice of Rannath serves his lord by cutting another tie with the mountains and making it less likely that more mountain folk will come here. That makes it more convenient for the few who remain in Carthon to go elsewhere – I wonder what happened to all the Lanarts? They used to hold land near Carthon,' he explained, 'and they were a sub-clan of the Altons, along with the Leyniers and the people of Syrtis. I hope the damned Dry-towners haven't killed them off by entangling them in blood feud and picking them off one at a time; they were good people. Domenic Lanart offered his eldest son in marriage to you, once, Melitta.'

'And you never told me.'

He chuckled. 'At the time you were eight years old.' Then he sobered again. 'I should have married you off, both of you, years gone; then we would have kinfolk at our call. But I was reluctant to part with you. Allira had no great wish to marry . . . '

They both fell silent. When they spoke again, it was of the past of Carthon and how it had fallen to this deserted state. Not until they were free of the city did Storn again broach the subject of their next move.

'Since Carthon has proved a false hope –'

Melitta broke in: 'We are within a few days' ride of Armida, and Valdir Alton has banded together all the men of the foothills against bandits – look what he did against Cyrillon des Trailles! Storn, appeal to him! Surely he will help us!'

'I cannot,' Storn said somberly, 'I dare not even meet with Valdir's men, Melitta. Valdir is a Comyn telepath, and has Alton powers; he would know at once what I have done. I think he already suspects. And besides' – he flushed darkly, ashamed – 'I stole a horse from one of Alton's men.'

Melitta said dryly, 'I wondered where you got such a beauty.'

Storn's own thoughts ran bitter counterpoint. *Valdir's foster son pledged himself with a knife – but it was to the Earthling, Barron. He knows nothing of me and has no friendship for me. And now that road is closed, too. What now?* He said at last, 'We are far kin to the House of Aldaran. I have heard that they, too, are a rallying-point for the people of the mountains. Perhaps they can help us. If they cannot help us for old kinship's sake, perhaps they will know where we can find mercenaries. We will go to Aldaran.'

Melitta, reflecting that meant recrossing the Kadarin and turning back into the mountains, wished they had gone there first; but then she remembered that Storn –

Barron – had come all the way from the valley lands far to the other side of the foothills. Carthon had been the best intermediary place they could locate, and furthermore Storn had had every reason to believe they could find help at Carthon. It was the strangest thing; when she did not look at him, it was easy to believe she rode with her brother Storn; the voice, unfamiliar in timbre and tone, and still her brother's familiar mannerisms and speech rhythms, as if it came filtered through distance. But when her eyes alighted on the strange figure which rode so easily on the great black horse – tall, dark, sullenly alien – the unease overtook her again. What would happen if Storn withdrew and she was left alone with this stranger, this off-worlder, this unbelievably alien man? Melitta had thought, after her terrible trek through the mountains, that she had little left to fear. She discovered that there were fears she had never thought of before this, the un-known hazards of an alien man, an alien mind.

She told herself, grimly, *Even if he – gets out – he couldn't be worse than Brynat's gang of toughs. I doubt if he'd want to murder me, or rape me.* Surreptitiously she studied the strange face, masked in her brother's familiar presence, and thought, *I wonder what he's really like? He seems a decent sort of man – no lines of cruelty, or dissipation – sad, if anything, and a little lonely. I wonder if I'll ever know?*

The third evening out of Carthon, they discovered that they were being followed.

Melitta sensed it first, with senses abnormally shar-pened by the tension and fear of the journey; as if, she was to say later, 'I'd gotten in the habit of riding looking over my shoulder.' She also suspected that she was developing, perhaps from contact with Storn or from some other stimulus, from a latent telepath into an actual one. She could not at first tell whether it was by the impact on her mind, or through some subliminal stimulation of her five sharpened senses – sounds too faint to be normally heard, shapes too distant to see – in any case it made little or no difference. When they found shelter in an abandoned herdsman's hut on a hill pasture, she finally told Storn of her suspicions, half afraid he would laugh.

Nothing was further from his mind than laughter. His mouth pinched tight – Melitta knew the gesture if not the mouth – and he said, 'I thought so, last night; but I thought I listened only to my own fear.'

'But who could be following us? Certainly none of Brynat's men, at such a distance! Men from Carthon?'

'That's not impossible,' Storn said. 'The House of Rannath might not mind seeing another of the old mountain families disappear – but then, sooner or later he might have to deal with Brynat's raiders himself. Raiding parties have been known to come as far as Carthon, and I dare say he would find us more towardly neighbors than the Scarface – he might not help us, but I doubt if he would hinder. No, what I fear is worse than that.'

'Bandits? A raiding nonhuman band?'

Somberly, Storn shook his head. Then, seeing Melitta's fear, he tried to smile. 'I'm no doubt imagining things, *breda*, and in any case we are armed.'

He did not say what he most feared: that Larry, through sworn friendship and fear for Barron, might have set Valdir on his track. He had not meant any harm – quite the opposite. But Barron had twice – or was it three times – asked questions about Carthon. It would have been simple enough to trail him there. And if no Terran had come there – well, Valdir at least would know what he had done and why Barron the Earthling had vanished. From what little Storn knew of the Comyn, once on the track of such an offense against the ancient laws of Darkover, they would make little of chasing him over half a world.

And when they caught him – what then?

With the uncanny habit she was developing, of reading his thoughts (Had he done well, to waken *laran* in the girl?) Melitta asked, 'Storn, just what *are* the Comyn?'

'That's like asking what the mountains are. Originally there were seven Great Houses on Darkover, or Domains, each with a particular telepathic gift. If I ever knew which House had which Gift, I have forgotten, and in any case, generations of inbreeding and intermarriage have blurred them so that nobody knows any more. When men spoke of the Comyn, they usually meant Comyn Council – a hierarchy of gifted telepaths from every House, who were responsible, first, for surveillance over the use of the old powers and gifts of the mind – and later, they gained temporal power, too. You've heard the ballads – originally the seven houses were descended from the sons of Hastur and Cassilda, so they say. It might even be true, for all I know, but that's beside the point. Just now, they're the givers of law – such law as there has been since the Compact – all over this part of Darkover. Their writ doesn't run in the Dry Towns, or in trailman country, and the mountain people are pretty much out of their orbit – you know as well as I do that we mountain people live under our own customs and ways.'

'They rule? Doesn't the King rule in the lowlands?'

'Oh, yes, there is a King in Thendara, ruling under the Comyn Council. The kingship used to rest with the Hasturs, but they gave it up, a few generations ago, in favor of another Comyn family, the Elhalyns, who are so intermarried with the Hasturs that it doesn't make much difference. You know all this, damn it, I remember telling you when you were a child, as well as about the Aldarans.'

'I'm sorry, it all seemed very far away.' They sat on blankets and furs inside the dark hut, crouched close to the fire, although to anyone accustomed to the fierce cold of the mountains it was not really cold. Outside, sleety rain whispered thickly along the slats of the hut. 'What about the Aldarans? Surely they're Comyn too?'

'They used to be; they may have some Comyn powers. But they were kicked out of Comyn Council generations ago; the story goes that they did something so horrible nobody knows or remembers what it was. Personally I suspect it was the usual sort of political dogfight, but I can't say. No one alive knows, except maybe the Lords of Comyn Council.' He fell silent again. It was not Comyn he feared, but Valdir, specifically, and that too-knowing, all-reading gaze.

Storn did not have to be told how Melitta felt about

what he had done. He felt the same way himself. He, too, had been brought up in the reverence of this Darkovan law against interfering with another human mind. Yet he justified himself fiercely, with the desperation of the law-abiding and peaceful man turned renegade. *I don't care what laws I have broken, it was my sister and my young brother in the hands of those men, and the village folk who have served my family for generations. Let me see them free and I don't care if they hang me! What good is an invalid's life, anyhow? I've never been more than half alive, before this!*

He was intensely aware of Melitta, half-kneeling before the low fire, close to him on the blankets. Isolated by the conditions of his life, as he had been till now, there had been few women, and none of his own caste, about whom he could care personally. To a developing telepath that had meant much. Habit and low vitality had made him indifferent to this deprivation; but the strange and newly vigorous body, in which he now felt quite at home, was more than marginally aware of the closeness of the girl.

It crossed his mind that Melitta was extraordinarily beautiful, even in the worn and stained riding clothes she had resumed when they left Carthon. She had loosened her hair and removed the outer cloak and tunic; under it was a loose rough linen shift. Some small ornament gleamed at her throat and her feet were bare. Storn, weary from days of riding, was still conscious of the reflex physical stir of awareness and desire. He let himself play at random with the thought, perhaps because all his other thoughts were too disturbing. Sexual liaisons between even full siblings in the mountains were not prohibited, although children born to such couples were thought unfortunate – the isolated mountain people were too aware of the dangers of inbreeding. With the grimmest humor he had yet felt, Storn thought, *In a stranger's body even that would not be anything to fear!*

Then he felt a sudden revulsion. The stranger's body was that of an alien, an Earthling, a stranger on their world – and he had been thinking of letting such a one share the body of his sister, a Lady of Storn? He set his jaw roughly, reached out and covered the fire.

'It's late,' he said. 'We have far to travel tomorrow. You'd better go to sleep.'

Melitta obeyed without a word, rolling herself in her fur cloak and turning away from him. She was aware of what he was thinking, and intensely sorry for him, but she dared not offer him overt sympathy. Her brother would have rejected it as he had done all her life, and she was still a little afraid of the stranger. It was not the low-keyed throb of his desire, which Melitta could feel almost as a physical presence, which disturbed her, of course. She did not care about that. As with any mountain girl of her caste, she knew that, travelling alone with any man, such a problem would in all probability arise. With Storn's own person she might not have thought of it, but she was much more aware of the stranger than Storn realized. She had been forced to think about this eventuality and to make up her mind about it. She felt no particular attraction to the stranger, although if his presence had been uncomplicated by the eerie uncanniness of knowing that he was also her brother, she might have found him intriguing; certainly he was handsome, and seemed gentle and from the tones of his voice, likable. But if she had even inadvertently roused desire in him, common decency, by the code of women of her caste, demanded that she give it some release; to refuse this would have been wrong and cruelly whorish. If she had been unalterably opposed to this possibility, she would not have agreed to travel entirely alone with him; no mountain girl would have done so. It would not have been impossible to find a travelling companion in Carthon.

In any case, it seemed that at the moment the matter was not imminent, and Melitta was relieved. It might have been entirely too uncanny; *like lying with a ghost,* she thought, and slept.

It was still dark when Storn's hand on her shoulder roused her, and when they saddled their horses and began to ride down the dark mountain path, they rode through still-heavy sleet which only after an hour or more of riding turned into the light rain which presaged dawn at this latitude and season. Melitta, cold and shivering, and even a little resentful, did not protest; she simply wrapped her cloak over her face as they rode. Storn turned into an inordinately steep and forsaken path, dismounted and led her horse along the slippery path through the trees until it was safe to ride again. She was thinking, *If it is Comyn on our trail, we may not be able to lose them. But if not, perhaps we can shake off our followers.*

'And we may gain two or three days' ride on them this way, if they are not accustomed to the mountain roads – they or their horses,' Storn said, out of nothing, and Melitta understood.

All that day and the next they rode through steeper and steeper mountain paths, with storms gathering over the heights, and at night they were too exhausted to do more than swallow a few mouthfuls of food and roll, half asleep already, into their blankets. On the morning of the third day after they had first sensed that they were followed, Melitta woke without any uneasy sense of a presence overshadowing their moves, and sensed that they had lost their followers, at least for the moment.

'We should reach Aldaran today,' said Storn, as they saddled, 'and if what I've heard is true, perhaps even the Comyn don't care to come this far into the hills. They may be sacrosanct in the lowlands, but not here.'

As soon as the mist cleared they sighted the castle from a peak, a gray and craggy height enfolded and half invisible in the hills; but it took them the rest of the day to approach the foot of the mountain on which it stood, and as they turned into the road – well-travelled and strongly surfaced – which led upward to the castle, they were intercepted by two cloaked men. They were asked their business with the utmost courtesy but nevertheless entreated to remain until the Lord of Aldaran knew of their coming, with so much insistence that neither Storn nor Melitta wanted to protest.

'Inform the Lord of Aldaran,' said Storn, his voice sounding gray with weariness, 'that his far kinsmen of Storn, at High Windward, seek shelter, counsel and hospitality. We have ridden far and are weary and call on him in the name of kin to give us rest here.'

'Rest in safety is yours at the asking,' said the man with exquisite courtesy, and Melitta sighed relief; they were among people of familiar ways. 'Will you wait in the gate house, my lord and *damisela?* I will have your horses looked to. I cannot disturb the Lord of Aldaran without his consent, but if you are his kinfolk, I am sure you need not wait long. I am at your service, and there is food for all travellers if you are in need of it.'

Waiting in the bare, small gate house, Storn smiled briefly at Melitta; 'Aldaran keeps the old ways of courtesy to strangers, whatever else may have befallen his household.'

In an almost unbelievably brief time (Storn wondered if some signaling device had been used, for there hardly seemed time for a messenger to come and go to the castle on the heights) the guard returned: 'The Lady Desideria bids me conduct you to the main house and make you welcome, Lord and Lady; and when you are rested and refreshed she will receive you.'

Storn murmured to Melitta, as they climbed the path and the steps leading upward, 'I have no idea who the Lady Desideria is. Old Kermiac would hardly have married; I suspect it is one of his son's wives.'

But the young woman who greeted them was no man's wife. She could hardly have been more than fifteen years old. She was a striking red-haired beauty whose poise and self-confidence made Melitta feel shy, countrified, and ill at ease.

'I am Desideria Leynier,' she said. 'My foster mother and my guardian are not at home; they will return tomorrow and give you a proper welcome.' She came and took Melitta's hands in her own, searching her face with gentle eyes. 'Poor child, you look tired almost to death; a night's sleep before you face your hosts will do you good; and you too, Master, you must rest and not stand on ceremony. The Storns are unknown to me but not to my household. I give you welcome.'

Storn returned thanks, but Melitta was not listening to the formal words. In the presence of this queerly self-possessed child, she sensed something more than poise; an awareness, an inner strength, and the touch of an uncannily developed sensitivity, so far beyond her own as to make her feel like a child. She made a deep reverence. '*Vai leronis,*' she whispered, using the ancient word for a sorceress wise in the old skills.

Desideria smiled merrily. 'Why, no,' she said. 'Only one, perhaps, who has a little knowledge of the old crafts – and if I read rightly, child, you are no stranger to them! But we can talk of that another time, I wished only to give you welcome in my foster parents' name.' She summoned a servant to conduct them, and herself went before them along the long halls. It was evidently a busy hour before the evening meal; people went back and forth in the halls, including some tall thin men whose presence and careless regard made Storn draw breath and clamp his fingers hard on Melitta's arm.

'There are Terrans here – this deep in the mountains,' he whispered, 'what in the name of Zandru's hells is going on here at Aldaran? Have we walked from the trap to the cook pot? I would not believe that any Terran alive had ever come into these mountains. And the girl is a telepath – Melitta, keep your wits about you!'

Desideria turned Storn over to a servant and conducted Melitta into a small room at the top of a tower, one of four tiny pie-shaped rooms on that level. 'I am sorry the accommodations are not more luxurious,' she apologized, 'but there are a great many of us here. I will send you wash water, and a maid to dress you, and although you would be more than welcome in the hall, child, I think you would be better to have dinner here in your room, and go to bed at once; without rest you will be ill.'

Melitta agreed gratefully, glad that she need not face so many strangers tonight. Desideria said, 'He is a strange man – your brother,' but the words held no hint of a prying question. She pressed Melitta's hands and kissed her cheek. 'Now rest well,' she said in that oddly adult way, 'and don't be afraid of anything. My sister and I are near you in the rooms across the hallway.' She went away. Left alone, Melitta took off her dirty and cold riding clothes and gratefully accepted the services of the quiet, incurious maid who came to wait on her. After bathing and eating the light, delicious food brought to her, she lay down in the soft bed and for the first time since the alarm bell had pealed Brynat's presence at the walls of Storn, she felt she could sleep in peace. They were safe.

Where is Storn? Is he, too, enjoying the luxury of safety and rest? Surely he must be mistaken about Terrans here. And it's surely strange — to find a vai leronis *deep in the mountains.*

—— 12 ——

Storm woke in the early light, and for a few minutes had no notion of where he might be. Around him were unfamiliar airs and voices, and he lay with his eyes closed, trying to orient himself, hearing footsteps ringing on stone, the sound of animals calling out for food, and strange voices rising and falling. They were peaceful morning sounds, not the sounds of a home in the hands of conquerors, and then memory flooded back and he knew he was in Castle Aldaran. He opened his eyes.

A curious apprehension lay on him, he did not know why. He began to wonder how long he could keep the upper hands over Barron — if it would be long enough to carry through his aims before he lost hold and found himself back in his own body, lying helpless in trance, guarded against personal attack but still unable to do anything for his family and his people. If that happened, he had no illusions about what would happen, sooner or later. Barron would go his own way, confused by a period of amnesia or perhaps false memories — Storm really did not know what happened to a man in Barron's position — and Melitta would be left alone without anyone. He would never know what happened to her in that case, he supposed.

And he did not want to return to his own body, blinded and helplessly imprisoned. If he did, what would happen to Barron, an Earthman alone in these strange mountains? For the very sake of his victim, he must maintain hold at all costs.

If there *were* Terrans at Castle Aldaran, what could it mean? Sick with unanswered and unanswerable questions, he flung back the covers and went to the window. Whatever happened in the end, he would enjoy these few days of sight out of a lifetime in darkness. Even if these days were his last.

From the window he looked down at the commotion in the courtyard. Men were going to and fro with an indefinable sense of purposiveness; there were Terrans among them, a few even in the leather dress of the spaceports – *how do I know that when I see it, never having been there?* – and after he had watched a while there was a stir among the men. One man and two uniformed attendants rode through the gate.

The man was tall, dark-bearded, well past middle age, and had an air of authority which reminded Storn vaguely of Valdir, although this man was clearly one of the mountain people. Storn realized from the hubbub surrounding him that he must be looking down at the arrival of the Lord of Aldaran. In a few hours he must face this man and ask for his help. Deep depression lay on Storn, for no discernible reason. Could even a whole army, if Aldaran were willing to put it at his disposal (and why should he?) dislodge Brynat? Storn Castle had been besieged before and it had never even been necessary to defend it. *Now that Brynat holds it, could anyone retake it? Army? We would need a god.*

The scene below melted away and Storn seemed to see within himself the great chained shape of Sharra, flame-crowned, golden-chained, beautiful and awesome. It was the vision he had seen when he lay helpless and blind behind the magnetic force-field at Storn Castle, his body tranced, his mind free ranging time and space in search of help from *somewhere*.

Sharra again! What does the vision mean?

Melitta came for him late in the forenoon with Desideria, who told them that her guardian was ready to receive them. As he followed the girls down the long corridors, stairs and hallways, Storn was quietly evaluating the poise, the strength and the obvious telepathic awareness of this very young girl, and coming up with a disquieting answer. She must be a Keeper – one of the young girls trained from infancy to work with the old matrix crystals and screens which would have made the few things at Storn Castle look like children's toys. But, overhearing snatches of conversation between them – Desideria seemed to have taken a fancy to Melitta, and talked to her freely – he gathered that there were four of them. In the old days a matrix circle, isolated from the world and giving all their time to it, had barely managed to train one Keeper in about ten years. If Aldaran had managed to train four in the few years since Storn had been here last, what was going on in this place?

But when he asked her a random question, using the polite form of address, *leronis*, Desideria gave him a merry smile and shook her head. 'No, my friend, I am not a *leronis*; my guardian does not like the word and its connotations of sorcery. I have been trained in a skill which anyone can learn who is a good telepath, just as anyone who is strong and fit enough can learn hawking or riding. Our world has accepted foolish ideas like sorcery for all too many years. Call me, if you like, a matrix technician. My sisters and I have learned this skill, far better than most; but there is no need to look at me with reverence because I have learned well!'

She went on looking at him with a girlish, ingenuous smile, then suddenly shivered, flushed and dropped her eyes. When she spoke again it was to Melitta, almost pointedly ignoring Storn.

He thought with a certain grimness, *Training or not, she is still conventional in the old ways – and I owe my life to that. If she were old enough to look at it that way – a trained telepath of her caliber need only look at me to know what I have done. Only the convention that girls of her age may not initiate any contact with men other than their blood kin, has saved me so far.*

The thought was strangely poignant – that this young girl of his mountain people, of his own kind and caste, and trained in all those things which had been the major solace of his life, was so guarded against him – and that he dared not reach out to her, mind or body. He felt as if he could have wept. He set his lips hard and followed the girls. He did not speak again.

Aldaran received them, not in a formal audience

chamber but in a small, friendly room low in the castle. He embraced Storn, calling him cousin, kissed Melitta on the forehead with a kinsman's privilege, offered them wine and sweets, and made them sit beside him; then he asked what had brought them there.

'It is far too long since any of your kinsmen have visited us at Aldaran; you live as isolated at High Windward as eagles in their aerie. It has come to mind in the last year or so that I have neglected kinship's dues and that I should ride to Storn, there is much astir in the mountains these days, and no one of our people should hold himself aloof too far; our world's future depends on it. But more of that later, if you are interested. Tell me what brings you to Aldaran, kinsman? How can I help you?'

He listened to their story gravely, with a gradually darkening and distressful face. When they had finished, he spoke with deep regret.

'I am ashamed,' he said, 'that I offered you no help before this, to prevent such a thing. For now it has happened, I am powerless to help you. I have kept no fighting men here for more than thirty years. Storn; I have kept peace here and tried to prevent feuds and raids rather than repelling them. We mountain people have been torn by feuds and little wars far too long; we have let ourselves go back to barbarian days.'

'I, too, had no fighting men and wanted peace,' Storn said bitterly, 'and all I gained from it was Brynat's men at my outworks.'

'I have Terran guards here and they are armed with off-world weapons,' Aldaran said. 'Would-be invaders knew enough, after a time or two, to let us alone.'

'With – weapons? Force weapons? But what of the Compact?' Melitta gasped in genuine horror. The law which banned, on this world, any weapon beyond the arm's reach of the wielder, was even more reverenced than the taboo against meddling with the mind. Aldaran said quietly, 'That law has delivered us to petty wars, feuds, murders and assassins. We need new laws, not stupid reference for old ones. I have broken the Darkovan code and as a result, the Hasturs and the Comyn hold my family in horror; but we are at peace here and we have no hooligans at our doors, waiting for an old man to weaken so that he can be challenged and set down as if the stronger swordsman were the better man. The law of brute force means only the rule of the brute.'

'And other worlds, I believe,' Melitta said, 'have found that unrestricted changes in weapons leads to an endless race for better and better weapons in a chase to disaster which can destroy not only men, but worlds.'

'That may even be true,' Aldaran said, 'and yet look what has happened to Darkover, in the hands of the Terrans? What have we done? We refused their technology, their weapons, we insisted on refusing real contact with them. Since the Years of Chaos, when we lost all of our own technologies except for the few in the hands of the Comyn, we've slipped back further and further into barbarism. In the lowlands, the Seven Domains keep their old rule as if no ships had ever put forth into space. And here in the mountains we allow ourselves to be harassed by bandits because we are afraid to fight them. Someone must step beyond this deadlock, and I have tried to do so. I have made a compact with the Terrans; they will teach us their ways and defenses and I will teach them ours. And as a result of a generation of peace and freedom from casual bandits and learning to think as the Terrans think – that everything which happens can and must be explained and measured – I have even rediscovered many of our old Darkovan ways; you need not think we are totally committed to becoming part of Terra. For instance, I have learned how to train telepaths of matrix work without the old superstitious rituals; none of the Comyn will even try that. And as a result – but enough of that. I can see that you are not in any state to think about abstract ideas of progress, science and culture as yet.'

'But what all this fine-sounding talks means,' said Storn bitterly, 'is that my sister and brother, and all my people, must lie at the mercy of bandits because you prefer not to be entangled in feuds.'

128

'My dear boy!' Aldaran looked aghast. 'The gods help me; if I had the means to do so, I would forget my ethics and come to your aid – blood kin is not mountain-berry wine! But I have no fighting men at all, and few weapons, and such as I have could not be moved over the mountains.' Storn was enough of a telepath to know that his distress was very real. Aldaran said, 'We live in bad times, Storn; no culture ever changed without people getting hurt, and it is your ill-fortune that you are one of those who are getting hurt in the change. But take heart; you are alive and unhurt, and your sister is here, and believe me, you shall be made welcome here as kin; this is your home, from this very day forth. The gods seize me, if I am not as a father to you both from this moment.'

'And my sister? My brother? My people?'

'Perhaps some day we will find a way to help them; some day all these mountain bandits must be wiped out, but we have neither the means nor any way.'

He dismissed them, tenderly. 'Think it over. Let me do what I can for you; you certainly must not return to throw your lives after theirs. Do you think that your people really want you to share their fate now that you have escaped?'

Storn's thoughts ran bitter counterpoint as they left Aldaran. Perhaps what Aldaran said made sense in the long run, in the history of Darkover, in the annals of a world. But he was interested in the short run, in his own people and the annals of his own time. Taking the long view inevitably meant being callous to how many people were hurt. If he had had no hope of outside help, he would gladly have sent Melitta to safety, if nothing more could be salvaged, and been glad there was a home for her here. But now that hope had been raised for more, this seemed like utter failure.

He heard, as from a distance, Desideria saying to Melitta, 'Something draws me to your brother – I don't know; he is not a man whose looks I admire, it is something beyond that – I wish I could help you. I can do much, and in the old days, the powers of the trained telepaths of

Darkover could be used against intruders and invaders. But not alone.'

Melitta said, 'Don't think we are ungrateful for your guardian's good will, Desideria. But we must return to Storn even if all we can do is to share the fate of those there. But we will not do that unless all hope is gone, even if we must rouse the peasants with their pitchforks and the forge folk of the hills!'

Desideria stopped dead in the hallway. She said, 'The forge folk of the caverns in the Hellers? Do you mean the old folk who worshipped the goddess, Sharra?'

'Indeed they did. But those altars are long cold and profaned.'

'Then I can help you!' Desideria's eyes glowed. 'Do you think an altar matters? Listen, Melitta, you know, a little, what my training has been? Well, one of the – the powers we have learned to raise here is that associated with Sharra. In the old days, Sharra was a power in this world; the Comyn sealed the gates against raising that power, because of various dangers, but we have found the way, a little – but Melitta, if you can find me even fifty men who once believed in Sharra, I could – I could level the gates of Storn Castle, I could burn Brynat's men alive about him.'

'I don't understand,' said Storn, caught in spite of himself. 'Why do you need worshippers?'

'And you a telepath yourself, I dare you, Storn! Look – the linked minds of the worshippers, in a shared belief, create a tangible force, a strength, to give power to that – that force, the power which comes through the gates of the other dimension into this world. It is the Form of Fire. I can call it up alone, but it has no power without someone to give it strength. I have the matrixes to open that gate. But with those who had once worshipped – '

Storn thought he knew what she meant. He had discovered forces which could be raised, which he could not handle alone, and with Brynat at his gates. He had thought, *If I had help, someone trained in these ways –*

He said, 'Will Aldaran allow this?'

Desideria looked adult and self-sufficient. She said,

'When anyone has my training and my strength, she does not ask for leave to do what she feels right. I have said I will help you; my guardian would not gainsay me – and I would not give him the right to do so.'

'And I thought you a child,' Storm said.

'No one can endure the training I have had and remain a child,' Desideria said. She looked into his eyes and colored, but she did not flinch from his gaze. 'Some day I will read the strangeness in you, Loran of Storm. That will be for another time; now your mind is elsewhere.' Briefly she touched his hand, then colored again and turned away. 'Don't think me bold.'

Touched, Storm had no answer. Fear and uncertainty caught him again. If these people felt no horror of breaking the Darkovan League's most solemn law, the Compact against weapons, would they have any compunctions about what he had done? He did not know whether he felt relieved or vaguely shocked at the thought that they might accept it as part of a necessity, without worrying about the dubious ethics involved.

He forced such thoughts from his mind. For the moment it was enough that Desideria thought there was a way to help. It was a desperate chance, but he was desperate enough for any gamble, whatever that might be – even Sharra.

'Come with me to the room where my sisters and I work,' she said. 'We must find the proper instruments and – you may as well call them talismans, if you like. And if you, Storm, have experimented with these things, then the sight of a matrix laboratory may interest you. Come. And then we can leave within the hour, if you wish.'

She led the way along a flight of stairs and past glowing blue beacons in the hallways which Storm, although he had never seen them before, recognized. They were the force beacons, the warning signs. He had some of them in his own castle and had experimented until he had learned many of their secrets. They had given him the impregnable field which protected his body and had turned Brynat's weapon, and the magnetic currents which guided the mechanical birds that allowed him to experience the sensation of flight. There were other things with less practical application, and he wanted to ask Desideria question after question. But he was haunted by apprehension, a sense of time running out; Melitta must have sensed it too, for she dropped back a step with unease.

He tried to smile. 'Nothing. It's a little overwhelming to learn that these – these toys with which I spent my childhood can be a science of this magnitude.'

Time is running out . . .

Desideria swung back a curtain, and stepped through a blue magnetic shimmer. Melitta followed, Storn, seized by indefinable reluctance, hesitated, then stepped forward.

A stinging shock ran through him, and – for an instant Dan Barron, bewildered, half-maddened, and fighting for sanity, stared around him at the weird trappings of the matrix laboratory, as if waking from a long, long nightmare.

'Storn – ?' Desideria's hand touched his. He forced himself to awareness and smiled. 'Sorry. I'm not used to fields quite as strong.'

'I should have warned you. But if you could not come through the field you would not have enough knowledge to help us, in any case. Here, let me find what I need.'

She flicked a small button and motioned them to seats. 'Wait for me.'

Slowly, Storn became aware of the strange disorganizing humming. Melitta was staring at him in astonishment and dismay but it took all his strength not to dissolve beneath the strange invisible sound, not to vanish . . .

A telepathic damper. Barron had been aware of one, at Armida, with his developing powers, he had just been disturbed at it, but now . . . now . . .

Now there was not even time to cry out, it was vibrating through his brain – through temporal lobes and nerves, creating disruption of the nets that held him in domination, freeing – Barron! He felt himself spinning through indefinable, blue-tinged, timeless space – falling, disappearing, dying – blind, deafened, entranced . . . He spun down into unconsciousness, his last thought was not of Melitta left alone, nor of his victim Barron. It was Desideria's gray eyes and the indefinable touch of her compassion and knowledge, that went down with him into the night of an unconsciousness so complete that it was like death . . .

Barron came to consciousness as if surfacing from a long, deep dive.

'What the bloody hell is going on here?' For a moment he had no idea whether or not he had spoken the words aloud. His head hurt and he recognized the invisible humming vibration that Valdir Alton had called a telepathic damper – that was all his world for a moment.

Slowly he found his feet and his balance. It was as if for days he had walked through a nightmare, conscious, but unable to do anything but what he did – as if some other person walked in his body and directed his actions while he watched in astonishment from somewhere, powerless to intervene. He suddenly woke with the controlling power gone, yet the nightmare went on. The girl he had seen in the dream was there, staring up at him in mild concern – his sister? *Damn it, no, that was the other guy.* He could remember everything he had done and said, almost everything he had *thought*, while Storn commanded him. He had not shifted position but somehow the focus had changed. He was himself again, Dan Barron, not Storn.

He opened his mouth to raise hell, to demand explanations and give a few, to make everything very clear, when he saw Melitta looking up at him in concern and faint fright. Melitta! He hadn't asked to get involved with her, but here she was and from what he could realize, he was her only protector. *She's been so brave; she's come so far for help, and here it is within her reach; and what will happen if I make myself known?*

He was no expert on Darkovan law and custom, but the one thing he did know from walking with Storn for seven or eight days was that, by Darkovan standards, what

Storn had done was a crime. *Fine – I could murder him for it, and God willing, some day I will. That's one hell of a thing to do to a man's mind and body!* But none of it was Melitta's fault. *No. I'll have to play the game for a while.*

The silence had lasted too long. Melitta said, with growing fear in her voice, 'Storn?'

He made himself smile at her and then found it didn't take an effort. He said, trying to remember how Storn had spoken, 'It's all right, that – telepathic damper upset me a little.' *And boy, was that a masterpiece of understatement!*

Desideria came back to them before Melitta could answer, carrying various things wrapped in a length of silk. She said, 'I must go and make arrangements for transportation and escort to take you into the hills near High Windward, to the caves where the forge folk have gone. You cannot help in this, why not go and rest? You have a long journey behind and ahead, and difficult things – ' She glanced up at Barron and quickly away, and he vaguely wondered why. *What's the matter with the red-headed kid?* He suddenly felt faint and swayed, and Desideria said quickly, 'Go with your brother, Melitta; I have many plans to make. I will come for you at sunset.'

Too disoriented and confused to do anything else, Barron let Melitta lead him through the suddenly strange corridors to a room where he knew he had slept the night before but which he had never consciously seen before. She stood looking down at him, distressed.

'Storn, what's happened? Are you ill? You look at me so strangely – *Storn! Loran!'* Her voice rose in sudden panic, and Barron put out a hand to quiet her.

'Take it easy, kid – ' He realized he was speaking his own language and shifted back, with some effort into the tongue Storn and his sister spoke together. 'Melitta, I'm sorry,' he said with an effort, but her eyes were fixed on him in growing horror and understanding.

'The telepathic damper,' she whispered. 'Now I understand. *Who are you?'*

His admiration and respect for the girl suddenly grew. This must have been just about the most terrifying and disconcerting thing that had ever happened to her. After she'd been so far, and been through so much, and with help so near, to find that her brother was gone and she was alone with a stranger – a stranger who might be raving mad, or a homicidal maniac, and in any case was probably mad – and she didn't run or scream or yell for help. She stood there white as a sheet, but she stood up to him and asked, 'Who are you?'

God, what a girl!

He said, trying to match her calm, 'I think your brother told you my name, but in case he didn't, it's Dan Barron. Dan will do, but you'd better go on calling me Storn or some of these people may get wise. You don't want that to happen when you've been through so much, do you?'

She said, almost incredulous, 'You mean – after what my brother's done to you, you'll still help me? You'll go back with us to Storn?'

'Lady,' said Barron, grim and meaning it more than he had ever meant anything in his life, 'Storn is the one place on this damn planet that I want to go more than anything else in the world. I've got to help you get those bandits out of your castle so that I can get to your brother – and when I get my hands on him, he's going to wish he only had Brynat Scarface to deal with! But that's nothing against *you*. So relax. I'll help you play your game – and Storn and I can settle our private difficulties later on. Good enough?'

She smiled at him, setting her chin courageously.

'Good enough.'

13

There was an airplane.

Barron looked at it in amazement and dismay. He would have sworn that there were few surface craft on Darkover; certainly no fuel was exported from the Zone for them, and he had never known of one being sold on Darkover, except one or two in Trade City. But here it was, and obviously of Empire manufacture. When he climbed into it he realized that all the controls had been ripped out; in place of an instrument panel was one of those blue crystals. Desideria took her place before it, looking like a child, and Barron felt like saying, 'Hey, are *you* going to fly this thing?' But he held himself back. The girl seemed to know what she was doing, and after what he had seen on Darkover, he wouldn't put anything past them. A technology which could displace possession by another mind was worth looking into. He began to wonder if any Terran Empire man knew anything about Darkover.

Melitta was afraid to climb into the strange contrivance until Desideria comforted and reassured her; then, looking as if she were taking her life in her hands and didn't care, she climbed in, resolved not to show her fear.

The queer craft took off in an eerie silence. Desideria put on another of the telepathic dampers inside, saying almost in apology, 'I'm sorry – I must control the crystal with my own strength and I dare not have random thoughts intruding.' Barron had all he could do to endure the vibrations. He was beginning to guess what they were. If telepathic power were a vibration, the damper was a scrambler to protect the user of the force from any intruding vibrations.

He found himself wondering what Storn would have thought of covering in a few hours, the terrain which he and Melitta had covered so laboriously, on foot and horse-back, in several days. The thought was unwelcome in the extreme. He did not want to think about Storn's feelings. Nevertheless, his beliefs about the backwardness of Dark-over had been gravely shaken in the last few hours. Their refusal of weapons other than knife and sword now seemed an ethical point – and yet Aldaran, too, seemed to have a valid ethical point, that this kept them struggling in small wars and feuds which depended for their success on who had the stronger physical strength.

But don't all wars depend ultimately on that? Surely you don't believe that rightness of a cause would mean that the right side would be able to get the biggest weapons? Would the feud between Brynat and Storn be easier settled if both of them had guns?

And if this was an ethical point rather than a lack of know-ledge, was it just possible that their lack of transit, manufacturing and the like might come from preference rather than lack of ability?

Damn it, why am I worrying about Darkovan ways when my own problems are so pressing?

He had deserted his work with Valdir Alton's men at the fire station. He – or Storn in his body – had stolen a valuable riding horse. He had probably irredeemably ruined himself with the Terran authorities, who had exerted themselves to give him this job, and his career was probably at a permanent standstill. He'd be lucky not to find himself on the first ship off Darkover.

Then it struck him that probably he need not go. The Empire might not believe his story but the Altons, who were telepaths, certainly would. And Larry had given him friendship, while Valdir was interested in the field of his professional competence. Perhaps there would be work for him here. He suddenly faced the awareness that he didn't want to leave Darkover and that he had at last become caught up in the struggles and problems of these people whose lives he had entered against his will.

I could kill Storn for what he did – but damn it, I'm glad it happened.

But this was the briefest flash of insight, and it disappeared again, leaving him lost and bewildered. During the days as Storn he had grown used to Melitta's companionship. Now she seemed strange and aloof and when he tried to reach out and touch her with his mind, it was an almost automatic movement and the low-keyed vibration of the telepathic damper interfered, making him feel dull, sick and miserable. He had expected to feel more at home flying then riding horseback but after a short time all he wished was that the flight would be over. Melitta would not look at him.

That was the worst of it. He longed for the flight to be over so that he could speak to her, touch her. She was the only familiar thing in this world and he ached to be near her.

Inconsistently, he was distressed when the flight ended and Desideria brought the craft expertly down in a small valley as quietly as a hovercraft. She apologized to Melitta for not coming nearer to Storn, but explained that the air currents around the peaks were violent enough to crash any small craft. Barron wondered how a girl her age knew about air currents. *Oh hell, she's evidently something special in the way of telepaths, she probably feels 'em through her skin or her balance centers or something.*

Barron had no idea where they were. Since Storn had never seen the place – being blind – Storn's memories were no good to Barron. But Melitta knew. She took charge, directing them toward a mountain village where Darkovans swarmed out, welcoming Melitta with delight, and showing Desideria a reverential awe which seemed to confuse the young girl – the first time Barron had seen Desideria taken aback – and even make her angry.

'I *hate* this,' she told him, and Barron knew she still thought she spoke to Storn. 'In the old days there might have been some reason for treating the Keepers like goddesses. But now we know how to train them, there is no *reason* for it – no more than for worshipping an expert blacksmith because of his skill!'

'Speaking of blacksmiths,' said Barron, 'how are we going to round up these forge people?'

She looked at him sharply and it was like the first time she had seen him. She started to say, 'You and Melitta will have to manage that; I have never been among them,' and stopped, frowning. She said, almost in a whisper and less to Barron than herself, 'You have changed, Storn. Something has happened –' and very abruptly turned away.

He had almost forgotten that to her he was still Storn. Elsewhere the masquerade was over; the village people ignored him. He realized that if these were people who lived near High Windward, they would know all the Storns.

He did not try to follow what Melitta was saying to the villagers. He was definitely excess baggage on this trip and he couldn't even imagine why Melitta had wanted him to come back to Storn with her. After a time she came back to Storn and Desideria, saying, 'They will provide horses and guides to the caverns of the forge folk in the hills. But we should start at once; Brynat's men patrol the villages every day or two – especially since I escaped – just to make sure that nothing is happening down here; and if it were known that they had helped me – well, I don't want to bring reprisals on them.'

They started within the hour. Barron rode silently close to Melitta, but he didn't try to talk to her. There was some comfort in her mere presence, but he knew that she felt ill at ease with him and he did not force himself on her. It was enough to be near her. He spared a thought for Storn, and this time he pitied him. *Poor devil, to have come so far and been through so much and then be forced offstage for the last act.*

He supposed Storn was lying entranced, high in his old wing of the castle, and if he was conscious at all – which Barron doubted – not knowing what had happened. *Hell, that's a worse punishment than anything I could do to him!*

He had been riding without paying much attention to where he was going, letting the horse choose his own road. Now the air began to be filled with the faintly acrid smell of smoke. Barron, alert from his days at the fire station, raised his head to sniff the wind, but the others rode on without paying attention.

Only Melitta sensed his attention and dropped back to ride at his side. 'It's not fire. We are nearing the caverns of the forge people; you smell the fires of their forges.'

They rode up along a narrow trail that led into the heart of the mountains. After a while Barron began to see dark caves lining the trail. At their entrances, small, swart faces peeped out fearfully. There were little men dressed in furs and leather, women in fur cloaks who turned shyly away from the strangers, and wrapped in fur, miniature children who looked like little teddy-bears. At last they came to a cavern gaping like a great maw, and here Melitta and Desideria alighted, their guides standing close to them in a mixture of fear and dogged protectiveness.

Three men in leather aprons, bearing long metal staves and with metal hammers, thrust into their belts – hammers of such weight that Barron did not think he could have lifted them – strode out of the cavern toward Melitta. Behind them the fearful people came up and gathered, surrounding them. The three men were dark, gnarled, short of stature but with long and powerful arms. They made deep bows to the women. Barron they ignored, as he had expected. The central one, with white patches in his dark hair, began to speak; the language was *Cahuenga*, but the pronunciation so guttural and strange that Barron could follow only one word in three. He gathered, however, that they were making Melitta welcome and paying Desideria almost more reverence than the village people had done.

There followed a long colloquy. Melitta spoke. It was a long speech that sounded eloquent, but Barron did not understand. He was very weary, and very apprehensive without knowing why, and this kept him from the attempt to reach out and understand as he had done with Larry and Valdir. *How the devil have I picked up telepathic gifts anyhow? Contact with Storn?* Then the white-haired forge man spoke. His was a long chanting speech that sounded wild and musical, with many bows; again and again Barron caught the word *Sharra*. Then Desideria spoke, and again Barron heard *Sharra*, repeated again and again, to cries and nods from the little people gathered around them. Finally there was a great outcry and all the little people drew knives, hammers, and swords and flourished them in the air. Barron, remembering the Dry-towners, quailed, but Melitta stood firm and fearless and he realized it was an acclamation, not a threat.

Rain was drizzling down thinly, and the little people gathered around and led them into the cavern.

It was airy and spacious, lighted partly by torches burning in niches in the walls, and partly by beautifully luminescent cystals set to magnify the firelight. Exquisitely worked metal objects were everywhere, but Barron had no leisure to examine them. He drew up beside Melitta as they walked through the lighted carven corridors, and asked in a low voice, 'What's all the shouting about?'

'The Old One of the forge folk has agreed to help us,' Melitta said. 'I promised him, in turn, that the altars of Sharra should be restored throughout the mountains, and that they should be permitted to return, unmolested, to their old places and villages. Are you weary from riding? I am, but somehow – ' she spread her hands, helplessly. 'It's been so long, and now we are near the end – we will start for Storn, two hours before the dawn, so that when Brynat wakes we will surround the castle – if only we are in time!' She was trembling, and moved as if to lean on him, then straightened her back proudly and stood away. She said, almost to herself, 'I cannot expect you to care. What can we do for you, when this is over, to make up for meddling in your life this way?'

Barron started to say, 'I do care, I care about you, Melitta,' but she had already drawn away from him and hurried after Desideria.

With jewel lights and with music provided by small, caged tree frogs and singing crickets, there was a banquet that evening in the great lower hall. Barron, though he could eat little, sat in wonder at the silver dishes – silver was commoner than glass in the mountains – and the jewelled, prismed lamps which played unendingly on the pale, smoke-stained walls of the cave. The forge people sang deep-throated, wild songs in a four-noted scale with a strangely incessant rhythm, like the pounding of hammers. But Barron could not eat the food, or understand a word of the endless epics, and he was relieved when the company dissolved early – he could understand enough of their dialect to know that they were being dismissed against the ride before dawn – and one of their guides took them to cubicles carved in rock.

Barron was alone; he had seen Melitta and Desideria being conducted to a cubicle nearby. In the little rock room, hardly more than a closet, he found a comfortable bed of furs laid on a bed frame of silver, woven with leather straps. He lay down and expected to sleep from sheer exhaustion. But sleep would not come.

He felt disoriented and lonely. Perhaps he had grown used to Storn's presence and his thoughts. Melitta, too, had withdrawn from him and he was inexpressibly alone without her presence to reach out to, in that indefinable way. He reflected that he had changed. He had always been alone and had never wanted it any other way. The rare women he had had, had never made an impression on him; they came, were used for the brief emotional release they could provide and were forgotten. He had no close friends, only business associates. He had lived on this world and never known or cared how it differed from Terra or from any other Empire planet.

Soon it would be over, and he did not know where he would go. He wished suddenly that he had been more responsive to Larry's proffered friendship; but then, Storn had spoiled that contact for him, probably for all time. He had never known what it was to have a friend, but then he had never known or realized the depths of his aloneness, either.

The room seemed to be swelling up and receding, the

142

lights wavering. He could sense thoughts floating in the air around him, beating on him, he felt physically sick with their impact. He lay on the bed and clutched it, feeling the room tipping and swaying and wondering if he would slide off. Fear seized him; was Storn reaching out for his mind again? He could *see* Storn, without knowing how it was Storn – fair, soft-handed and soft-faced, lying asleep on a bier of silks – face remote and his human presence simply not there at all. Then he saw a great white bird, swooping from the heights of the castle, circling it with a strange musical, mechanical cry and then sweeping away with a great beating of wings.

The room kept shifting and tipping, and he clung to the bed frame, fighting the sickness and disorientation that threatened to tear him apart. He heard himself cry out, unable to keep back the cry; he squeezed his eyes tight, curled himself into a fetal position and tried hard not to think or feel at all.

He never knew how long he lay curled there in rejection, but after what seemed a long and very dreadful time he came slowly to the awareness that someone was calling his name, very softly.

'Dan! Dan, it's Melitta – it's all right; try to take my hand, touch me – it's all right. I would have come before if I had known – '

He made an effort to close his fingers on hers. Her hand seemed a single stable point in the unbelievably shifting, flowing, swimming perspective of the room, and he clung to it as a man cast adrift in space clings to a magnetic line.

He whispered, 'Sorry – room's going round . . . '

'I know. I've had it; all telepaths get this at some time during the development of their powers, but it usually comes in adolescence; you're a late developer and it's more serious. We call it threshold sickness. It isn't serious, it won't hurt you, but it's very frightening. I know. Hold on to me; you'll be all right.'

Gradually, clinging to her small hard fingers, Barron got the world right-side up again. The dizzy disorientation remained, but Melitta was solid, a firm presence and not wholly a physical one, in the midst of the shifting and flowing space.

'Try, whenever this happens, to fix your mind on something solid and real.'

'*You* are real,' he whispered. 'You're the only real thing I've ever known.'

'I know.' Her voice was very soft. She bent close to him and touched her lips gently to his. She remained there, and the warmth of her was like a growing point of light and stability in the shifting dark. Barron was coming quickly back. At last he drew a deep breath and forced himself to release her.

'You shouldn't be here. If Desideria discovers you are gone –'

'What would it be to her? She could have done more for you; she is a Keeper, a trained telepath, and I – but I forgot, you don't know the sort of training they have. The Keepers – their whole minds and bodies become caught up into the work they do – must keep aloof and safeguard themselves from emotions –' She laughed, a soft, stifled laugh and said, almost weeping, 'Besides, Desideria doesn't know it, but she and Storn –'

She broke off. Barron did not care, he was not interested in Desideria at the moment. She came close to him, the only warm and real thing in his world, the only thing he cared about or ever could . . .

He whispered, shaken to the depths, half sobbing, 'And to think I might never have known you –'

She murmured, 'We would have found one another. From the ends of the world; from the ends of the universe of stars. We belong together.'

And then she took him against her, and he was lost in awareness of her, and his last thought, before all thought was lost, was that he had been a stranger on his own world and that now an alien girl from an alien world had made him feel at home.

14

They started two hours before dawn in a heavy snowfall; after a short time of riding the forge folk on their thickset ponies looked like polar bears, their furred garments and the shaggy coats of the ponies being covered with the white flakes. Barron rode close to Melitta, but they did not speak, nor need to. Their new awareness of one another went too deep for words. But he could feel her fear – the growing preoccupation and sense of desperation in what they were about to dare.

Valdir had said that the worship of Sharra was forbidden a long time ago, and Larry had been at some pains to explain that the gods on Darkover were tangible forces. *What was going to happen? The defiance of an old law must be a serious thing – Melitta's no coward, and she's scared almost out of her wits.*

Desideria rode alone at the head of the file. She was an oddly small, straight and somehow pitiable little figure, and Barron could sense without analyzing the isolation of the one who must handle these unbelievable forces.

When they came through the pass and sighted Storn Castle on the height, a great, grim mass which he had never seen before, he realized that he had seen it once through Storn's eyes – the magical vision of Storn, flying in the strange magnetic net which bound his mind to the mechanical bird.

Had I dreamed that?

Melitta reached out and clasped his hand. She said, her voice shaky, 'There it is. If we're only in time – Storn, Edric, Allira – I wonder if they're even still alive?'

Barron clasped her hand, without speaking. *Even if you*

have no one else, you will always have me, beloved.

She smiled faintly, but did not speak.

The forge folk were dismounting now, moving stealthily, under cover of the darkness and crags, up the path toward the great, closed gates of Storn. Barron, between Desideria and Melitta, moved quietly with them, wondering what was going to happen which could make both Melitta and Desideria turn white with terror. Melitta whispered, 'It's a chance, at least,' and was silent again, clinging to his hand.

Time was moving strangely again for Barron; he had no idea whether it was ten minutes or two hours that he climbed at Melitta's side, but they stood shrouded by shadows in the lee of the gates. The sky was beginning to turn crimson around the eastern peaks. At last the great, pale-red disc of the sun came over the mountain. Desideria, looking around her at the small, swart men clustered about her, drew a deep breath and said, 'We had better begin.'

Melitta glanced up uneasily at the heights and said, her voice shaking, 'I suppose Brynat has sentries up there. As soon as he finds out we're down here, there will be – arrows and things.'

'We had better not give him the chance,' Desideria agreed. She motioned the forge folk close around her, and gave low-voiced instructions which Barron found that he could understand, even though she spoke that harsh and barbarian language. 'Gather close around me; don't move or speak; keep your eyes on the fire.'

She turned her eyes on Barron, looking troubled and a little afraid. She said, 'I am sorry, it will have to be you, although you are not a worshipper of Sharra. If I had realized what had happened, I would have brought another trained telepath with me; Melitta is not strong enough. 'You' – suddenly he noticed that she had neither looked directly at him, nor spoken his name, that day – 'must serve at the pole of power.'

Barron began to protest that he didn't know anything about this sort of thing, and she cut him off curtly. 'Stand here, between me and the men; see yourself as gathering all the force of their feelings and emotion and pouring it out in my direction. Don't tell me you can't do it. I've been trained for eight years to judge these things, and I know you can if you don't lose your nerve. If you do, we're probably all dead, so don't be surprised, whatever you see or whatever happens. Just keep your mind concentrated on me.' As if moved on strings, Barron found himself moving to the place she indicated, yet he knew she was not controlling him. Rather, his will was in accord with hers, and he moved as she thought.

With a final, tense look upward at the blank wall of the castle, she motioned to Melitta.

'Melitta, make fire.'

From the silk-wrapped bundle she carried, Desideria took a large blue crystal. It was as large as a child's fist, and many-faceted, with strange fires and metallic ribbons of light. It looked molten, despite the crystalline facets, as she held it between her hands, and it seemed to change form, the color and light within it shifting and playing.

Melitta struck fire from her tinderbox; it flared up between her hands. Desideria motioned to her to drop the blazing fragment of tinder at her feet. Barron watched, expecting it to go out. Desideria's serious, white face was bent on the blue crystal with a taut intensity; her mouth was drawn, her nostrils pinched and white. The blue light from the crystal seemed to grow, to play around her, to reflect on her – and now, instead of falling, the fire was rising, blazing up until its lights reflected crimson with the blue on Desideria's features – a strange darting, leaping flame.

Her eyes, gray and immense and somehow inhuman, met Barron's across the fire as if there were a visible line between them. He almost heard her voice within his mind. *'Remember!'*

Then he felt behind him an intense pressure beating up – it was the linked minds of the forge folk, beating on his. Desperately he struggled to control this new assault on his mind. He fought, out of control, his breath coming fast and his face contorted, for what seemed ages – though it was only seconds. The fire sagged and Desideria's face showed rage, fear and despair. Then Barron had it – it was like gathering up a handful of shining threads, swiftly splicing them into a rope and thrusting it toward Desideria. He almost felt her catch it, like a great meshing. The fire blazed up again, exuberantly. It dipped, wavered toward Desideria.

It enveloped her.

Barron gasped almost aloud and for a bare instant the rapport sagged, then he held fast. He knew, suddenly, that he dared not falter, or this strange magical fire of the mind would flare out of control and become ordinary fire that would consume Desideria. Desperately intense, he felt the indrawn sigh of the men behind him, the quality of their worship, as the fires played around the delicate girl who stood calmly in the bathing flames. Her body, her light dress, her loosely braided hair, seemed to flicker in the fires.

With a scrap of awareness on the edge of his consciousness, Barron heard shouts and cries from the wall above, but he dared not cast an eye upward. He held desperately to the rapport between the girl in the flames and the forge folk.

An arrow flew from nowhere; behind them someone cried out and an almost invisible thread broke and was gone, but Barron was barely conscious of it. He knew without full consciousness that something had roused the castle, that Brynat's men knew they were under strange attack. But his mind was fixed on Desideria.

There was a great surge of the flame, and a great shout from behind them. Desideria cried aloud in surprise and terror and wonder, and then – before Barron's eyes, her frail fire-clad figure seemed to grow immensely upward, to take on height, majesty and power. And then it was no delicate girl who stood there, but a great veiled Shape, towering to the very height of the outworks and castle, a woman in form, hair of dancing flame, tossing wildly on the wind, wrapped in garments of flame and with upraised arms from which dangled golden chains of fire.

A great sighing cry went up from forge folk and village people crowded behind them.

'Sharra! Sharra, flame-haired, flame-crowned, golden-chained – Sharra! Child of Fire!'

The great Shape towered there, laughing, tossing arms and long fiery locks in a wild exultation. Barron could feel the growing flood of power, the linked minds and emotions of the worshippers, pouring through him and into Desideria – into the flame-form, the Form of Fire.

Random thoughts spun dizzily at the edge of his mind. *Chains. Is this why they chain their women in the Dry Towns? The legends run, if Sharra ever broke her chains the world would explode in flame . . . There is an old saying on Terra that Fire is a good servant but a poor master. On Darkover too; every planet that knows fire has that byword. Larry! You! Where are you? Nowhere here; I speak to your mind, I will be with you later.*

He dropped back into rapport with Desideria, vaguely knowing he had never left it and that he was moving now outside normal time and space perception. Somehow Storn was there, too, but Barron shut out that perception, shut out everything but the lines of force almost visibly streaming from the worshippers – through his body and mind, and into the Form of Fire. With multiplied perception he could see into and through the Form of Fire – see Desideria there looking tense and quiet and frail and somehow exultant – but it was not with his eyes.

Arrows were flying into the crowd now, dropping off men who fell strangely rapt and without crying out. One arrow flew into the Form of Fire, burst into flame and vanished in soundless, white heat. The Form loomed higher and higher. There came a loud outcry from behind the castle walls as the great Form of Sharra stretched out arms with fingers extended – fingers from which ball fires and chain lightning dripped. The men on the walls shrieked insanely as their clothes burst into flame, as their bodies went up in the encompassing fire.

Barron never knew how long that strange and terrible

battled raged, for he spent it in a timeless world, beyond fatigue and beyond awareness, feeling it when Brynat, raving, tried to rally his fleeing, burning, dying men; sensing it when the great Form of Fire, with a single blow, broke the outworks as if they had been carved in cheese. Brynat, desperate, brave against even the magic he did not believe in to the very end, charged along the walls, beyond the reach of the flames.

From somewhere a great white bird came flying. It flapped insanely around Brynat's head; he flung up his arms to batter it away, while it flew closer, stabbing with its glittering metallic beak at his eyes. He lost his balance, with a great cry; tottered, shrieked and fell, with a long, wailing scream, into the ravine below the castle.

The fires sank and died. Barron felt the net of force thin and drop away. He realized that he was on his knees, as if physically battered down by the tremendous streams of force that had washed over him. Melitta stood fixed, dumbfounded, staring at the heights.

And Desideria, only a girl again – a small, fragile, red-haired and white-faced girl – was standing in the ring of the dying fire, trembling, her dress and hair unscorched. She gestured with her last strength and the fire flickered and went out. Spasmodically, she thrust the blue stone into the bosom of her dress; then she crumpled unconscious to the ground, and lay there as if dead.

Above them the great wall of the castle breached, with none left to resist them except the dying.

15

The forge folk picked up Desideria with reverent awe and carried her, through the break in the walls, inside the castle yard. They would have done the same to Barron, except that he made them put him down, and went to Melitta, who stood weak-kneed and white. The forge folk disposed of the dead simply, by tossing them into a deep chasm; after some time the wheeling of the *kyorebni*, the corbies and lammergeiers of Darkover, over the crags marked their resting place. In their enthusiasm they would have thrown the wounded and dying after them, but Barron prevented them and was astonished at the way in which his word was taken for law. When he had stopped them he wondered why he had done it; what was going to happen to these bandits now? There weren't any prisons on Darkover that he knew about, except for the equivalent of a brig, in Trade City, where unprovoked fighters and obstreperous drunks were put to cool off for second thoughts; anyone who committed a worse crime of violence either died in the attempt or killed anyone who might try to prevent him. Perhaps Darkover would have to think about penalties less than death, and he frankly wished Alderan the joy of the task.

At Melitta's orders they went down into the dungeon and freed young Edric of Storn, whom Barron found, to his surprise and consternation, to be a boy of fifteen. The terrible wounds he had sustained in the siege were healing, but Barron realized with dismay that the child would bear the scars, and go lame all his life. He welcomed his rescuers with the courtly phrases of a young king, then broke down and sobbed helplessly in Melitta's arms.

Allira, numbed and incoherent with terror – she had not known whether they were being rescued or attacked by someone eager to replace Brynat – they found hiding in the Royal Suite. Barron, who had formed a strange picture of her from Melitta's thoughts, found her to be a tall, fair-haired, quiet girl – to most eyes more beautiful than Melitta – who came quickly back from terror. With dignity and strength, she came to thank their helpers and place herself at their service, and then to devote herself to reviving and comforting Desideria.

Barron was almost numb with fatigue, but he was too tense to relax even for an instant. He thought, *I'm tired and hungry, I wish they'd bring on the victory feast or something,* but he knew firmly in his mind, *This isn't the end. There's more to come, damn it.*

He realized with disbelief that the sun had risen less then thirty degrees above the horizon; the whole dreadful battle had been over in little more than an hour.

The great white bird, glittering as if formed of jewels that shone through the feathers, swooped low over him; it seemed to be urging him upward. Melitta behind him, clutching at his hand, he climbed the long stairs. He passed through the archway, through the blue tingle of the magnetic field and into the room where the silken bier lay. On it lay the form of a man – sleeping, tranced or dead – like a pale statue, motionless. The bird fluttered above it; suddenly flapped and dropped askew to the floor, lying there in a limp dead tangle of feathers gleaming with jewels like some broken mechanical toy.

Storn opened blind eyes and sat up, stretching out his hand to them in welcome.

Melitta flew to him, clasping her arms around his neck, laughing and crying at once. She started to tell him, but he smiled bleakly. 'I saw it all – through the bird's eyes – the last thing I shall ever see.' He said, 'Where is Barron?'

Barron said, 'I am here, Storn.' He had felt that at this moment he would be ready to kill the man; now he felt all his rage and fury drain out of him. He had been a part of this man for days. He could not hate him or even resent him. What could he do to a blind man, a frail invalid? Storn was saying in a low voice, ridden with something like shame, 'I owe it all to you. I owe everything to you. But I have suffered for it – and I will take whatever comes.'

Barron did not know what to say. He said roughly, 'Time enough to settle that later, and it won't be me you have to settle it with.'

Storn rose, leaning heavily on Melitta, and took a few fumbling steps. Barron wondered if he were lame, along with everything else, but Storn sensed the thought and said, 'No, only stiff from prolonged trance. Where is Desideria?'

'I am here,' she said from behind them, and came forward to take his hand.

He said, almost in a whisper, 'I would have liked to see your face once, only once, with my own eyes.' He fell silent with a sigh. Barron had no longer any anger against Storn, only pity; and he knew, with that new expanded awareness that was never to leave him, that his pity was the worst revenge he could have taken on the man who had stolen his work, his body, and his soul.

A horn sounded far below them in the courtyard, and the women rushed to the window. Barron did not have to follow them. He knew what had happened. Valdir Alton, with Larry and his men, had arrived. He had followed them through half the mountains, and when he lost them, had come directly here, knowing that sooner or later, it must end here. Barron no longer wondered how his masquerade had been known for Storn. Larry had been in rapport with him too long for any surprise.

Storn drew himself upright, with a quiet assumption of courage that did much to dilute the pity and redeem him in Barron's eyes. 'My punishment is in Comyn hands,' he said, almost to himself. 'Come, I must go and welcome my guests – and my judges.'

'Judge you? Punish you?' Valdir said, hours later, when formalities were over. 'How could *I* punish you worse than the fate you have brought on yourself. Loran of

Storm? From freedom you are bound, from sight, you are blind again. Did you really think it was only to protect their victims that we made what you have done our greatest taboo?'

Barron had found it hard to face Valdir; now, before the man's hard justice, he looked directly at him and said, 'Among other things, I owe you for a horse.'

Valdir said quietly. 'Keep it. His identical twin and stable mate was being trained for my quest gift to you when you had finished your work among us; I shall bestow him upon Gwynn instead. I know you were not responsible for leaving us so abruptly, and we have you – or Storn,' he smiled faintly, 'to thank for saving the entire station, and all the horses, the night of the Ghost Wind.'

He turned to Desideria and his eyes were more severe. He said: 'Did you know that we had laid Sharra, centuries ago?'

'Yes,' she flared at him, 'your people in the Comyn would rob us both of Terra's new powers – and Dark-over's old ones.'

He shook his head. 'I am not happy with what the Aldarans are doing. But then, I am not entirely happy with what my own people are doing, either. I do not like the idea that Terra and Darkover shall always be the irresis-tible force and immovable object. We are brother worlds; we should be joined – and instead – the battle between us is joined. All I can say is – God help you, Desideria – any god you can find! And you know the law. You have involved yourself in a private feud and stirred up telepathic power in two who did not have it; now you, and you alone, are responsible for teaching your – victims – to guard them-selves. You will have little leisure for your work as a Keeper, Desideria. Storn, Melitta and Barron are your responsibility now. They must be trained to use the powers you broke open in them.'

'It was not I all alone,' she said, 'Storn disovered these things on his own – and it will be my joy, not my burden, to help him!' She glared at Valdir defiantly, and took Storn's pale hands between her own.

Larry turned to Barron, with a glance at Valdir as if asking permission. He said, 'You still have work with us. You need not return to the Terran Zone unless you like – and, forgive me, I think you have no place there now.'

Barron said, 'I don't think I ever did.' Melitta did not move, but nevertheless he felt as if Melitta had come to stand beside him, as he said, 'I've never belonged anywhere but here.'

In a queer flash he saw a strange divided future; a Terran working both for and against Terra on this curiously divided world, torn relentlessly and yet knowing where he belonged. Storn had robbed him of his body and in return had given him a heart and a home.

He knew that this would always be his place; that if Storn had taken his place, he would take Storn's, increasingly with the years. He would master the new world, seeing it through doubled eyes. The Darkover they knew would be a different world. But with Melitta beside him, he had no fears about it; it was a good world – it was his own.